PRAISE FOR *LAST SEEN*

"A fine, intelligent, deceptively simple piece of work."
The Montreal Gazette

"*Last Seen* is vintage Matt Cohen. . . . In [his] skilled
hands, grief transforms to magic and joy."
Greg Hollingshead

"An offbeat, wise book about obsessive grieving
and the pull life exerts at the edge of the grave."
The Globe and Mail, Top Ten Books of 1996

"*Last Seen* shows that Cohen is capable of touching lyricism . . . and
that his fine writing style is matched by an equally fine mind."
Books in Canada

"A dark, mordantly funny novel [and] a story of
tremendous emotional power."
The Edmonton Journal

"*Last Seen* poses the old question — how can we bear the mortality
of those we love — in a remarkable new way. When Alec loses his
brother Harold, difficult and marvellous events begin to overtake
him on the wintery streets of Toronto. This is a wonderfully
intelligent, adventurous and, dare I say it, funny book.
Wit and feeling go hand in hand on every page."
Margot Livesey

"Moving and trenchantly funny, it may well be the best of the
Toronto writer's twelve novels . . . a kaleidoscopic study of
the complications of brotherly love and family."
Maclean's

Last Seen

Matt Cohen

A NOVEL

Vintage Canada
A Division of Random House of Canada

First Vintage Canada Edition, 1997

Canadian Cataloguing in Publication Data

Cohen, Matt, 1942-
   Last seen

ISBN: 0-676-97081-8

I. Title

PS8555.054L3 1997   C813'.54   C96-931044-7
PR9199.3.C65L3 1997

Text design: Gordon Robertson

Printed and bound in the United States of America

10 9 8 7 6 5 4 3 2 1

To Mum – Christmas '87

all my love
Ros

All the decisive blows are struck left-handed.

– Walter Benjamin

HAROLD had been dreaming comets. Incandescent fireballs swooping down on the sun. Now he was listening to the children in the back lane, the proud arcs of their voices, their shoes slapping and scuffing against the dirt. "Throw it! Come on, throw it!" His nose filled with the dark stained smell of his old baseball glove, deep and shining with oil and sweat, the sharp magic snap of burnished leather swallowing a hard-hit ball. The voices melted into laughter. Running. The chase. Voices raised in a chorus of objection. Silence or what would be silence if not for the sounds of cars, birds, a cup breaking just after his elbow nudged it from the bedside table.

"Shit."

"It's all right. Do you want your glasses?"

Harold opened his hands, got his glasses facing the right way, slid them over his nose.

"Is that better?"

"You can turn on the lights. I'm not tired."

There was the click of a light switch. But Francine had given him the wrong glasses, the reading glasses he used for the tiny print of legal documents and medicine bottles. They turned everything more than six inches away into a black fog, which was his situation now. He was immersed in a black fog punctuated by irregular glimmers that kept slipping away whenever he tried to focus on them. He breathed out slowly. The main thing was to relax and stay calm.

"I'm going to the bathroom," Harold said. He could picture the white cylinder with his contact lenses. It was on the little ledge beneath the mirror. He lifted the sheet. Waited for the pain in his back and shoulder to subside. Then inched his legs towards the side of the bed until his feet fell to the floor. As they did he rolled onto his side and pushed hard with his right arm, now his strongest even though he was left-handed.

Francine helped him to his feet. He allowed this. He also allowed her to walk him through the black fog to the bathroom. When they arrived he took hold of the door with his right hand, the stronger hand since the cancer had done something peculiar to his neck and left shoulder, and then he said, as he always did these days, "Excuse me while I shut the door in your face." Francine laughed. She was the only one who knew when he meant to be funny and when he was just too tired to care.

He closed the door, locked it, groped for his contacts. The container was in the place he'd remembered.

"I'm going to practise standing," he announced. Francine's laughter sent sheets of lightning through the darkness. Every time he took a whizz he had to find a different way to announce it. That was one of his games. When his father had been sick — before he made the miracle recovery that got him back to playing eighteen holes of golf and pontificating on the political problems of the country as though being resurrected made him infallible — his game had been mental arithmetic. Doctors, family and random visitors were encouraged to give him problems. You would go into the hospital room and whoever was there would be scribbling numbers on the back of an envelope, desperately trying to keep up with the quicksilver mind of Dr. Constantine, as everyone called him, former Gold Medal chemist, author of over a hundred scientific papers and still sharper than the needles they were using to keep him alive.

When Harold finished practising standing, he flushed the toilet. Then he turned back to the mirror, felt for his lenses, got one on a finger and tried to put it onto his right eyeball. His hand was steady but his head wouldn't stay in place. The mirror was giving off flashes of light but he couldn't see himself. Which was why he was here. He inhaled, exhaled slowly. When you've got a nest of snakes growing up your spinal cord, relaxing is not so simple. Finally he got the lens onto his eye. His eye filled with water. He reached for a towel and that was when he slipped. There was still enough of him left that his body thumped when it hit the floor.

"You all right?"

"No problem," Harold said. He was wedged against the toilet. His back was now rigid, his head pressed against the cold tiled wall. He finished putting in the contact lens. Then he got one hand around the towel rack and the other on the edge of the sink.

"You sure everything's okay?"

"Everything's perfect. Why don't you get me some coffee?"

"Decaffeinated?"

"Please. And maybe something to eat. A piece of toast." Francine would like that. Asking for food was a good sign.

"Do you want to try some home-made raspberry jam?"

"Did you make it yourself?"

"Of course," said Francine. "Wait until Thanksgiving. You haven't lived until you've had my cranberry sauce."

"I'll start with the jam," Harold said. "If I like it, I promise to live until Thanksgiving."

He listened to her footsteps go down the stairs and disappear into the kitchen. Then he gritted his teeth and pulled with all his strength. Nothing happened. He pulled again. This time he could feel himself lifting. But just as his bum came up off the floor, the towel rack ripped free. He fell back, twisted to one side while the snakes writhed in a wild dance that made him want to shriek. He bit his lips, allowed himself a small moan, waited for the snakes to coil back into their nest. The sweat was pouring out, but the good thing was he'd ended up with a towel across his face. He dropped the rack in the bathtub but kept the towel, carefully wiped himself dry. Then he realized that in twisting he had become unstuck. Using his heels he dragged himself forward and away from the toilet. Francine was calling up to ask if he wanted milk in his coffee. He shouted back. Then, as the microwave started to roar in the kitchen, he grunted again to expel the pain, crawled to the door, grabbed the handle, jerked himself to his feet.

Again his body poured out sweat, this time in relief and gratitude. Of all his escapes from near disaster, this surely was the most spectacular. An omen, finally, of good things to come.

By the time Francine was back with the coffee and toast he was sitting on the edge of the bed.

"You got here by yourself? I thought you were going to wait for me." She piled up the pillows so he would be able to sit comfortably, then helped him swing his feet up onto the bed. "Did you get your lenses in?"

"No problem." Now he felt the hot coffee cup bumping against his fingers. She must have been holding it out, waiting for him to take it. He opened his hands, closed them slowly, letting his fingers find the warm curve, the handle. He wondered how she could see so well in the dark. He could hear his own voice telling her once again to turn on the light.

"It's on," Francine said. Her weight on the bed, her fingers stroking his cheeks, circling his eyes.

He woke up with his hand on the morphine pump. Unseen voices crashing. "Shhhh," he whispered, freezing his body so that the voices would not be drowned by the rustle of his skin against the sheets. There was the high whistle of a car alarm, the electronic bird he'd learned to recognize these mornings. Door slamming. Engine coughing to life. The smooth roar of gas exploding in polished

steel. He ran his fingers along the top of the pump. As the
car passed his window he imagined himself standing on
his lawn, saw the rich black rubber of the tires digging into
the asphalt, felt his own toes grabbing sympathetically at
the wet grass. The feel of dew between his toes. The heavy
dew-soaked cuffs of his pyjamas. The soles of his bare feet
aching against the cold ground. The hollow blue sky an
open mouth, waiting to fill with sun and warmth. Now he
had the button beneath the index finger of his right hand.
With his left he was squeezing a bar of the hospital bed.
Squeezing hard. He sent his mind out to investigate. His
fingers were locked around the bar. The muscles of his
arm were rigid, his shoulder sore and aching. Being blind
didn't help. At first he had tried to remember. At first he
believed being blind was only a temporary inconvenience,
a freak accident caused by one of the brain tumours
pushing into the wrong nerve. Nothing eaten, nothing
gained. The skin on his finger had grown so thick he
could hardly feel the button any more. Or maybe they had
changed the button to a smaller one to make it harder to
find because he was pressing it too much. At first he tried
to remember everything as it used to be so that when his
tumour shrank and his eyes started to work again he
wouldn't be shocked or disappointed. People's faces. Who
had what colour eyes. His car, wherever it was. Towed
away or covered with dirt or rusting to nothing in the
garage of the house his parents used to own when he was
still in high school. That kind of thing happened. A car
you didn't drive could show up in some old garage where
you used to play, fall away to nothing. You wondered what

people thought, some kid coming out in the morning to find his bicycle and there's this old car shedding time and soon that's all you can see, discarded time, transparent as an October snakeskin.

Now he could feel his fingers. Also his back. He had been pretending the pain in his back was lying beside him, contained, fire in a balloon. But now it was loose, it wasn't fire any more; it was in his bones, whatever *it* was, a wild aching in the centre of his bones, his muscles, his nerves, everything going crazy trying to adjust to sudden tidal waves of pain.

Harold pressed the button. Once. Twice. Three times. Could feel his vein swell where the needle was taped to his belly as the morphine pushed in. Began to breathe from his belly, grunt and breathe like a woman in labour, a woman gripped by pain as unbearable as his own, a woman torn apart as the whole universe conspired to force a life out of her body, just as the life was being forced out of his.

Harold screamed. He listened to his voice as it flew from his mouth, echoed harshly in the room, swooped down the hall and spread through the house.

Hurrying footsteps. The smell of coffee. A familiar voice, warm and kind, attached to a face he would never see again. Whenever a new nurse arrived, Alec, the professional, provided the descriptions. But with Francine, Alec's help was the last thing he needed — her sun-coloured eyes, flushed cheeks, dark honey hair curled in tendrils around her ears — he didn't need to see Francine: he needed the river of her voice and most of all he needed her hands, the hands that were already on his neck, sliding down his back to find the pain, hands that knew how to follow his moans and writhings until they were at the source.

"How are you this morning?" asked Francine.

"Good," Harold said.

"Good. That's good. I like you to be good." Francine lifted his hand from the pump and rubbed his palm with hers, erasing the feel of metal and plastic, breathing colour and light into the swarming black shadows, heating his skin with hers, heating it to a glow until he could feel the life that the universe had forced out of him starting to flow back. And he, incredibly, was sucking it in. Blind, lame, crippled, constipated, riddled with cancer, soaked in drugs, he was happy to suck it in, suck in life. This was it. Life. Like the last drops of the world's greatest bottle of wine. Get it all.

She is in the room. He can hear the crackle of a book page turning. The slow rhythm of her breathing. The top of his head pressed against the wall, his feet constricted in this thing they call a hospital bed. This uncomfortable coffin with its crank that pushes him up and down, its barred sides that collapse noisily whenever they want to wash or change him. This coffin in the room where he used to sit on the couch watching baseball games, reading the stacks of magazines he loved to buy on his trips to New York or Paris — the room with the bookcases he'd built himself to store his favourite paperbacks back in the days of his first company, his first dog, his first power saw

ripping through the pine one fall afternoon until eventually he just sat on the floor drinking a beer and marvelling
at the sawdust suspended in the air, tiny naked wood frag-
ments floating in the gold October light. Magic forest.

"Do you want to play the game?" Francine asked.

He pushed the button. Nothing happened. He pushed
again. Still nothing. No more morphine. The pump was on
a time lock. Time to suffer until some clock he had never
seen was ready to release him. "How are you feeling?"

"Not bad."

"Good."

He jabbed down on the button, again and again.

"Do you want a shot?"

*For Christ's sake, yes, I want a shot. I want a hundred
shots.* He wanted to hear the saw-edge of his voice, his cutting words. He wanted to see people's faces jump, contract,
run away like scared rabbits at the bitter sounds he wanted
to make. He tried to jab the pump again but as he moved
his hand his shoulder flashed as though an axe had just
been driven into the bone and the only sound he heard
was a loud moan that tore at his own guts.

Francine's hand on his arm, promising. Then the needle's sharp hammer smashing into him. "Count to ten,"
Francine said.

Count to a million, Harold thought. *Count to a million,
a billion, a trillion.* He got a picture of numbers marching
through space, a long ticker-tape parade of glowing tiny
white numbers marching through the blackness and his
job was to call out each number as it passed until there
were no more numbers and then he would be dead.

"Are we playing the game?" she asked.

"I am."

The game was about trips he would take, or trips he and Francine might take together. Sometimes they played it silently, sometimes out loud. They would go down to the furnace and travel through the pumps and radiators to see who was inside making those strange sexy gurgling noises. Or to a restaurant in Paris. He couldn't remember its name, but at the next table had been a dog sitting on a green plaid blanket in the lap of an elderly lady who ate a huge dessert of meringue overflowing with brandied cream sauce. Venice. . . . Now the smooth steel bars of his coffin had fallen away and he was floating through the sky on his mattress. He could see the stars, hear the strange white jabberwocky of their connecting buzz, the hollow hum of the time machine, eternity clearing its throat, getting ready to swallow him down.

First Premonition:

DRIBBLING the basketball low and away from his body to avoid Harold's long arms, Alec skirts around his brother, puts the ball down one last time and then starts upward. Sees Harold's big hand, a giant five-fingered stop sign. So often, that big five-fingered sign has wrapped itself around the ball, taken it away from Alec. But this time Alec's leap towards the basket carries him past Harold's hand and, incredibly, floating above it, he finds himself looking down on Harold as he sends the ball against the backboard and into the net.

"Razzle dazzle," Harold says.

"Just a trick I learned in the navy," Alec replies. Then he drives by Harold again, again finds himself flying over his taller younger brother, whose eyes look somehow blurred and puzzled.

They are on an outdoor basketball court, a few minutes walk from Harold's house. Long ago, Harold had been a high school basketball star. The captain of the team. In the yearbook picture he stood in the centre of the front row, not the best player or the tallest, but the one who never gave up, the left-handed jump-shooter who liked to make a few unbelievable fakes before springing high into the air and sending a message of pure hope towards the basket. He was the one with the biggest grin, the shortest brushcut, the long musician's fingers wrapped around the ball.

They keep playing. True, they're no longer in high school. Harold has, Alec notes in his newly dominant role, the beginning of a belly. Gravity has become their barber. But still, didn't they play together just a couple of winters ago in an old-timers' league? Doesn't Alec still run every day, or at least every second or third day? Didn't he see Harold, just recently, lift something impossibly heavy?

They're walking home and Alec says to Harold, "Am I jumping higher or have you started to play on your knees?"

"My back's been bothering me," Harold says. Then he describes how the doctor has made him join a health club so he can exercise on the weight machines and build up his muscles. Alec listens. He never goes to the doctor except once or twice a year when he's convinced he's got cancer. The doctor tells him it's just a lump or a wart, or something she could clip off right now with a pair of nail scissors.

"So are you doing all that?" Alec asks.

Harold nods.

"You should get an x-ray or something," Alec says uncomfortably. "Maybe your vertebrae melted together from too much sex."

"They went all over me for the insurance," Harold replies. "Nothing wrong but the bad back."

Alec nods, relieved. He himself doesn't require business insurance because he has no business. As a part-time teacher, freelance writer of everything from magazine articles to television plays to quickly remaindered novels, of which one was translated into Polish, he has given up on ever receiving such amenities. He switches from worrying about Harold's health to worrying about the fact he has never dared to have a thorough check-up, though he certainly intends to.

Second Premonition:

A year later. Family weekend at camp. They have gone together to the camp they both attended as children — Alec for one year, Harold for five — to see Alec's children. Alec is approaching the water, feeling self-conscious about the pale underground colour of his skin, the way one leg has become more bowed than the other, a previously unnoticed roll of fat on his hips — in sum, the fact that he doesn't look like an eighteen-year-old lifeguard. His only consolation is that he never looked like an eighteen-year-old lifeguard. Harold is sitting on the edge of the dock, his shoulders bent forward. Harold once *was* an eighteen-year-old lifeguard — and swimming instructor. But now his skin is also white, though there's a bit of burn on his shoulders and neck. His moles are very visible against the whiteness of his skin. Alec can't help thinking Harold shouldn't expose himself to the sun this way. Harold turns and looks up at him, his eyebrows and moustache raised in that comical-quizzical way he has. He splashes his feet in the water.

Alec finds himself remembering another white skin incident. It was long ago: he had gone to visit his parents at a cottage they'd rented. It was a hot summer day; his father took off his shirt to absorb a little sun. His skin, Alec had noted with surprise, was now dotted with hundreds of mole-like freckles. Looking at his father in the sun, the incredible total collapse of his seventy-year-old belly and pectoral muscles, the eerily familiar frizz of hair across his chest and stomach, Alec had felt a strange mixture of pro-tectiveness and alarm.

The next day, when his mother made the ritual phone call to thank Alec for the visit, Alec had asked about the moles, and she had replied that they were a side-effect of one of the medications his father was taking. Alec was so relieved he had been tempted to ask if farting was another side-effect, since breaking wind in public places had recently arrived as a necessity. A few months later his father had a sudden stroke and died.

Looking now at Harold's moles, Alec remembered his father's. Later, when it was dark and he and Harold were down by the water having a beer and looking out to the island where they had camped decades before, Alec asked Harold if he was taking drugs for his back. "No," Harold replied, looking surprised.

The wind. The cold beer in his hand. The comfort of the water lapping onto his feet. The breeze through the pines that surrounded them. The shouts from the beach where the kitchen staff were now enjoying their after-dinner swim.

Alec thought Harold appeared distracted. The water, the wind in the pines, the moon that now sparkled across the lake — sure. But then there was work, there was money, there was the cellular telephone in the trunk of Harold's car.

"How *is* your back?" Alec found himself saying.

"It's all right."

"Doesn't bother you any more?"

Harold shrugged. "It bothers me. But I've read the books on back problems and they all say you have to learn to live with it."

"The problems."

"The pain."

"Does it hurt right now?"

"Not really."

That meant, Alec knew, that it did. It probably hurt a lot. Pain was not something Harold liked to think about, or admit to. Alec looked out across the water, watched the bats flitting out from the pines.

"You ever try aspirin? Painkillers?"

"All the time. Anti-inflammatories work better."

"Is your doctor any good?"

"The best."

Well, Alec wanted to say, *you're only thirty-six years old, you can't just go around with a sore back for the rest of your life*. And then remembered the look in Harold's eyes as he soared over him playing basketball.

Harold stood up. "Well," he announced, "that was nature." Eventually they ended up sitting in lawnchairs in the middle of a field, slathered in mega-smell bug repellent, drinking beer, smoking, swatting mosquitoes and watching for shooting stars while speculating on the mating habits behind the sounds they heard from nearby cabins.

A Moment of Reassurance:

Alec and Margaret are having a party. This is a rarity, a one-time anniversary special. The party is to take place up at the cabin, a ramshackle half-built warning to would-be city handymen that Alec bought and began piecing together just before he met Margaret.

To prepare for the party, Alec makes some space with his current third-hand lawnmower. The story of his lawnmowers is a separate sad tale caused by a combination of Alec's stinginess and the fact that his lawnmowers aren't used on lawn — there is none — but on whatever grass, sumac roots, small cherry or poplar saplings as well as other unidentified sticks, flowers or rocky outcroppings he can get at before he either shears off the blade, runs out of gas or is driven inside by blackflies.

Because of the unprecedented number of expected guests, he also creates a parking lot in the field below the cabin. This requires a combination of lawnmower, scythe and pruning shears, but in the end a dream-like field of green appears where once were swamp grass and thistles. Then, just like in the movie — a movie Alec saw with Harold — Harold appears. Alec watches him from the window and then, remembering Harold's bad back, goes down to help him with his things. Harold's colleague, ambiguously titled "friend" and "vice-president of everything", Nancy Prescott, is wearing a wide-brimmed white hat that makes a nice contrast with her sunglasses, especially in the slanted August light.

She waves at Alec and compliments him on the parking lot. Harold is at the back of the car. When he straightens up, Alec sees he is tanned and fit-looking, his arms corded with muscles straining with the weight of two picnic hampers, a case of beer, the black attaché case containing what he calls his "magic kit" — a bottle of grappa along with his collection of marked decks, weirdly weighted balls, collapsible hats, etc. — that he uses to keep children amazed and entertained.

Alec, realizing how concerned he'd been about Harold, finds himself babbling foolishly as he watches him carry everything up to the cabin, where, wiping his hands together, flexing his long fingers, grinning his big old grin, he demands a cold beer.

"What happened to your back?" Alec can't help asking.

"Back? What back?" Harold looks a lifetime younger. The children — Nancy's as well as Alec and Margaret's — are chasing after each other, Nancy and Margaret are talking about a movie they both saw; Alec is looking contentedly at his younger brother and seeing that while he was worrying Harold into some ridiculous illness, Harold has simply shrugged it all away. He is once again the yearbook team captain, Mr. Head Boy, Mr. Everything, back in his own movie of perfect health, cloudless future, a bottle of beer in one hand and the universe in the other. One day Alec will ask Harold why he doesn't carry fire insurance for his house. "Fire insurance?" Harold will say, amazed. "My house isn't going to burn down." That was just before the meteor crashed through the roof.

First Phone Call:

A year has passed since the party. Alec is about to go to a conference in Amsterdam to research a magazine article on a certain Dr. Herbert Franz Strauss Meyser. Fifteen years ago, Dr. Meyser was an obscure Dutch professor, and the supervisor for the thesis Alec never wrote. Now he is verging on star status and going about giving lectures based on the book that had attracted Alec to him in the first place — *White Men Dying* — a learned and witty denunciation of the white European male and everything he believes he has accomplished. To pass the time on the plane, Alec has bought the paperback of the latest John Updike novel featuring Rabbit Angstrom, the basketball-playing, used-car dealer whose anti-exploits Alec and Harold have been following since they were teenagers.

Reminded of Harold, Alec picks up the telephone thinking he will tell Harold he has this last Rabbit novel, and also about the trip he's about to take. He calls him at the office and Nancy answers. They talk for a moment. There is something in Nancy's voice, but then Alec has never been able to read Nancy.

"Is everything okay?" he asks, feeling guilty for prying.

"Sure," Nancy says, in a brittle voice that at first seems familiar, though annoyed.

"You know," Alec says, feeling that he needs to excuse himself for having asked such an unusual question, "I've been worrying about Harold's back. It really seemed to be bothering him for a while."

"It still is."

PARC NATIONAL DES
LACS WATERTON LAKES
NATIONAL PARK

30.06.2001

See Pass
Voir laissez-passer

GW:AD GR/DO:GR ADULTE   70.00
Pass/Laissez-passerO

Total   **70.00**
GST/TPS INCL   4.58
Cash/Comptant   70.00
11:55 Clerk 1   141
PARK GATE-MAIN

GST#/No de TPS:R101530723

Park Pass

Display on dashboard
with date showing
on driver's side

Laissez-passer

Placer sur le tableau
de bord du côté du
conducteur montrant
bien la date

Parks Canada

Parcs Canada

Canada

Thank you

Enjoy your visit

Merci

Bon séjour

Park Pass

Display on dashboard
with date showing
on driver's side

Laissez-passer

Placer sur le tableau
de bord du côté du
conducteur montrant
bien la date

Canada

"Maybe I should talk him into doing his exercises or something. Is he around?"

"He's gone to get his bicycle fixed."

"Great," Alec says. And then: "It can't be that bad, if he's riding a bicycle. I wouldn't want to ride a bicycle if I had a sore back."

"Actually, he took it in the car."

This time the panic in Nancy's voice surges unmistakably.

After putting the phone down Alec calls Margaret. "Something's wrong with Harold." Then he tells her about the phone call, Nancy's voice.

"They're probably having a money problem or something," Margaret says.

That night, lying in bed, just about to drift into sleep Alec hears the panic in Nancy's voice again. He wants to wake up Margaret, up but how can you interrupt someone's sleep to insist that a voice sounded strange on the telephone?

Second Phone Call:

Two days later, in Amsterdam: Alec is in his room in the Hotel Ambassade, overlooking a canal, feeling like a prince. This is it. World fame. Well, it isn't exactly world fame, or even local fame, but it's a week away from teaching and a free and luxurious return to a city he had once loved. He calls the office of Dr. Meyser but gets only a recorded message. He leaves a message of his own, then sits back to continue the Rabbit saga. Rabbit — alas, poor Rabbit — is now in his mid-fifties, swollen with decades of eating potato chips, slowed by hardening arteries and an overworked heart.

He seems like a mess for his age, Alec thinks, wondering if he and Harold, ten or twenty years hence, could also be dragged down so far by greasy potato chips and chocolate bars. There is a great description of Rabbit savouring an m&m as it melts in his mouth and the layers of chocolate give way to pure sweetness. Disgusting, Alec thinks. He had never liked m&m's and now he knew why.

The telephone rings. It is Harold. "I have bad news," he says.

"What's wrong?"

"Lung cancer."

A silence. More than a silence. A hole. Harold can't die, Alec thinks, that would be the worst thing ever.

"You *have* to get better," Alec says, and right away hates himself for saying such a stupid thing. Eventually he will learn that it doesn't matter if he says or thinks stupid things because, he will eventually learn, nothing he says or thinks can touch the silence, the hole, the black void of emptiness and fear which beginning now will only grow larger.

Then Alec is saying it again: "You have to get better, you *have* to get better."

"I know. I'll do my best." Harold is crying. Alec is crying. Alec is the older brother. He is the one who is supposed to be able to do what needs doing. To provide solace and relief. But all he can do is tell Harold that he *has* to get better. This is the worst, Alec is thinking, the *worst* that can happen, and another part of his mind is remembering

that he read somewhere, sometime, that a reasonable per-
centage of lung cancer victims survive for five years.

He asks Harold for the details. Behind what Harold is
saying, Alec hears something else in his brother's voice —
like what he heard in Nancy's — and then he asks if the
cancer has spread.

"There are a few other hot spots," Harold says.

"Where?"

"In the bones. The back."

Now Alec can't even pretend to fill the silence. This is
the worst, he keeps repeating to himself, wanting to vomit,
this is the *worst*. But he's still wrong. This is only the
beginning. The worst is something he would never be
able to imagine. None of his nightmares, his fears, his
hypochondria, the terrible scenes he has seen, read or
written, will have prepared him for the worst.

2

The next day, Alec flew home. Beside him sat a woman
returning to Canada to nurse her daughter through a
kidney transplant operation. Her name was Ruth Nilssen,
Danish by marriage, she explained, though her husband
had "passed away"; she was now living in Holland, where
she had been born, taking care of her elderly parents. Her
sick daughter was an identical twin, but amazingly the
other twin had no kidney problems and was available as a
donor. . . . Ruth Nilssen's eyes were china blue and as she
spoke, which was almost constantly, her fingers painfully

twisted themselves together, making each other splotchy as
they squeezed and pulled.

I also have my troubles, Alec thought of commiserat-
ing: my father who "passed away"; my sick brother who is
not my identical twin but is nonetheless essential, my
essential other, the only other member of the club of two
who grew up in the strange universe of our parents' house,
the blood relation whose blood is now poisoned. But the
longer Alec delayed saying anything, the more unsure he
was of where to start, and the more inexplicable he
thought it would seem to have waited one, then two, then
several hours to reveal his own terrible mission. Instead, he
listened and he ate and he drank. By the time the movie
started he was in another movie, his own movie.

Alec's movie had him in a hospital bed, preparing to
donate parts of his body to save Harold. He was filled with
terror, resentment, guilt about feeling terror and resentment. Margaret and the children were beside him. It was
the night before the operation. He sent Simon and Emily
to the cafeteria for a snack so he could have a few last words
with Margaret. Then, as the lights dimmed, he tried to
explain to Margaret why Harold's sickness threatened him
so much, attacked him at his very core, why Harold's strong
and vital body, inexplicably cracking under the pressure of
life, was a blow he could not absorb.

Alec had come out of the luggage area and passed
through customs when he saw Harold. He was wearing a
new yellow windbreaker and his hair was brushed back at the
sides. Pacing around nervously, his usual self, snapping his
fingers and looking at his watch. *Not so bad*, was Alec's first

thought, along with a rush of gratitude to Harold for coming, for knowing, for finding as always a moment to imagine what it was like to be the other person. Which was why Harold was the kind who met people at airports, remembered birthdays, paid equal attention to cousins and step-children.

After Harold died Alec found raw wires dangling in his basement, bills that had mouldered so long in their envelopes that the acid in the paper had eaten away the numbers. But Harold had found time to come to the airport and now, spotting Alec, he waved. Alec, exhausted by the tidal waves of dread and fear that had been washing through him, began moving forward. Each step revealed something new: the twenty pounds Harold had already lost; the dark stained hollows beneath his eyes; the way his pants bagged around his legs, legs that carried him stiffly.

"Good to see you," Harold finally said. "How are you?"

"I'm all right. How are *you*?"

"Not bad." On the way home Alec listened as Harold told him how the nurses had dressed in armour while pouring the first dose of his new, never-before-tried, super-powerful, last-ditch-desperation chemotherapy into his opened veins. "The amazing thing is," Harold concluded, "they say that one in twenty live, they just don't know why."

3

One November evening, a few months after Harold died, as Alec was drinking Scotch and settling down for a pre-bed read of the obituaries, the telephone rang.

"Smash-A-Cap, Incorporated," Alec answered. Margaret was already asleep, so he could talk this way. Otherwise, she monitored his public utterances for signs that he was overly depressed.

"Always on the job, I see," came Nancy Prescott's voice.

"Ah. Ms. Prescott. Calling for a little late-night dictation, I presume?"

"Go ahead, dictate. Then find someone to obey."

Nancy was still working at cleaning up the final details of the business. Their last campaign, designed for a beer manufacturer, had foundered as Harold grew sicker. The beer company had become impatient, had written Harold letters saying that just because he had cancer was no excuse for him to be late on an important contract. From there to the proposed — though unexecuted — Smash-A-Cap campaign had been a short distance.

Emptiness over the telephone.

"I was hoping you would come in tomorrow," Nancy said. "Lunch?"

The next day Alec met Nancy at the Lawrence Avenue restaurant where they all used to go during the first months of Harold's illness. Alec would arrive just before noon and sit with Harold in his office, watching him play solitaire on his computer, while Nancy fended off bill collectors or composed threatening letters to their own dead-beat accounts. At lunch time they would set off in a slow procession. Nancy and Harold walking ahead, while Alec followed. Cancer, chemotherapy and the cholesterol-free diet Harold had decided was necessary, had now stripped him of fifty pounds. His hair, too. As Alec followed behind, his brother looked to him like a long skinny-legged heron in too-big clothes, wearing a broad-brimmed hat which covered the top half of his newly naked head, itself wavering uneasily on his elongated neck.

At the restaurant the hat would stay on. Harold would order a tuna sandwich, no margarine. Nancy would have a salad and provide commentary on the conversation of the postmen who met daily for nourishment and a few drinks at the counter.

The prospects of Nancy's salads and his brother's tuna sandwich always made Alec want to order more substantially. Milk shakes, cheeseburgers, hot chicken sandwiches. The food would arrive and he'd wolf it down with fake enthusiasm, practically clapping between bites, while Harold and Nancy played with theirs. Harold's knuckles had also lost their hairs. As a result his fingers were now strangely white and graceful. Every time Alec looked at these new fingers he thought of the way Harold had taken classical guitar lessons for a few years, then mysteriously given them up. Before the cancer Harold's knuckle hairs had been thick and black; like everything else about him they'd given off an air of untouchable vitality. On a list of the hundred most likely people to get sick and die, even the thousand most likely, the *million* most likely, Harold would not have made an appearance. When it came to getting sick and dying, Harold just wasn't the type.

At first Alec had tried to worry his brother better. Whenever he was out walking he would find himself chanting beneath his breath, to the beat of his feet on the pavement, "Live, Harold, *live*. Live, Harold, *live*." In the afternoons after seeing Harold, he would go the Y where they used to play basketball, and change into his old cut-offs and the high-top sneakers Harold had spotted in a window as they struggled back to the office after one of their dismal lunches. "Buy them," Harold urged. "I'll be able to play with you next week, I promise."

Harold had come into the store with Alec and sat stiffly beside him while Alec tried on the various possibilities. "You'll fly in these," the clerk had said. "He needs them just to compete," Harold had joked, and in his dark broad-brimmed hat and his coat that now hung loosely from his shoulders, Harold looked like some diabolic Faustian coach supervising the miraculous resurrection of his star student.

But Harold was the one in need of resurrection. "My back is killing," Harold said the next week. He was starting a new medication for the pain. "Go ahead. You need the practice."

That day, and every free afternoon thereafter, Alec played basketball. My prayer, he would say to himself sardonically. In the deserted gym, while oblong shafts of light from the high windows made their magic patterns on the floor, Alec would bounce the basketball a few times, then start taking jump shots. When he'd warmed up he would bet, the way he used to with Harold, except that now he was betting for Harold's life: "Three in a row and he lives for five years guaranteed"; "Sink this hook shot and he feels no pain for a week"; "Left-handed lay-up means he'll be out here playing with me in six months."

In December, two weeks before Christmas, Alec came to Harold's office one day to find Harold sitting behind his desk, a big grin on his face, dictating a proposal into a cassette. Thrown carelessly onto the floor, the way it had been in the other life that Alec could hardly remember, was Harold's old gym bag.

"After lunch," Harold said, "if you have a minute, we could try a few hoops."

Alec called into the university to cancel his afternoon class, explaining that he had broken a tooth. They filed into the restaurant. Harold had his usual brown bread and tuna but Nancy splurged on a shrimp salad while Alec celebrated with a toasted chicken sandwich and a beer.

Harold removed his hat. Over the weeks a thin fuzz had begun to reappear on his skull. When he reached for the pepper his fingers trembled. In the old days Alec would have made a joke about people who couldn't even handle a pepper shaker hoping to handle a basketball. But now he just shifted his eyes away, hoping Harold didn't know he'd seen. On the way back from lunch Harold walked gingerly, as though his bones had declared war on each other. Each step seemed a trial. Outside the office Alec stopped at his car. Harold looked at it sadly, as though it was the car and not Alec he'd let down. As though he might never again come back from a tuna sandwich lunch, grab his stinking old gym bag, go down to the Y and sink a left-handed jump shot from centre court.

By January, Harold was only going to work two or three days a week. He still hadn't made it to the gym. Alec bought an answering machine and installed it in his basement office. One day he came home from his seminar to a message from Harold saying the doctor had ordered a new course of radiation treatments because he had started to see double. Alec went upstairs and poured himself as much Scotch as he could fit into a large glass. When the glass was empty he telephoned Margaret and told her Harold's cancer had spread to the brain. Then he sat in the kitchen and watched the sky until he couldn't stand it any more and went out for a walk.

He didn't call Harold back until that evening. When Harold picked up the phone Alec could hear music playing, the voices of friends. But Harold's voice was cold and distant. Alec apologized for interrupting. Harold made a sound that might have been a laugh. Alec offered to drive him to the hospital for his first treatment. "Don't worry," Harold said. "It's already taken care of."

Despite the treatments, the cancer got worse. April was the cruellest month. In April the pain grew so bad there was nothing else. Alec stopped going to the gym because his prayers weren't working, because he could no longer bear the thought of himself floating in mid-air, flicking the ball through the magic light towards the newly painted iron hoop, while Harold lay immobilized in the hospital bed they'd brought into the house, long white fingers curled round the shining steel bars.

Harold in the hospital bed, blind, one hand on his pump and the other curled around the bars. Harold free-associating on morphine, writhing in pain, slumped forward for one of Francine's massages.

Days Alec didn't spend at Harold's, he would stumble about checking his watch every few minutes to know where Harold was in his routine: baths, massages, visits from a "healer", the physiotherapist, various friends who had taken on rotating shifts, most of all Francine. Robotically Alec would drive the children to school. Sit in class trying to concentrate during the presentation of a paper. Absently mark papers or go the supermarket and crash the shopping cart through the aisles. When he got home he would go down to look at his answering machine, the red light blinking to signal messages he didn't want to hear.

April was the cruellest month, but May was worse. Sometimes, unable to stand it, Alec would drive up to the cabin for a few days and try to console himself with thoughts of spring. He would explain to Harold and Francine that he had an article to write, assignments to finish, a speech to give. Francine would listen sympathetically to his lies. "Do you have to go?" Harold would ask, meaning, it seemed to Alec: Can't you wait until I die? "Yes," Alec would reply, feeling like some Judas burying the knife in his own brother's back, some coward fleeing the battlefield where his comrades still lay. But he fled. And when he returned Harold would be worse.

"How was it?" Harold would ask.

"Got it done," Alec would say. As though such things could still matter. "How are you?"

"Not bad." Alec would look down at his brother's blind face, the face of the brother whose pain he could neither witness nor relieve, and his brother's face and lips would

twitch with anger and hopelessness and need. Then out
of desperation Alec would ask about Harold's next or last
visit to the doctor and Harold, who never wavered in the
conviction that he was getting better, would talk about
possible new treatments or the doctor's refusal to see the
obvious or his plans to enlarge the deck when summer
came.

Summer came. In mid-June Harold went into a coma for
two days. Alec talked to the doctor about ending things.
"It's not over yet," the doctor said. As though there was a
secret meter only she could hear ticking. When Harold
came to he asked for a cup of coffee, decaf, one milk, one
sugar, and wanted to know if he'd missed the baseball
game. Alec accepted an invitation to a five-day conference
on "Post-Semiotic Journalism" at the University of British
Columbia. He didn't tell Harold he was leaving. Francine
pretended to agree that Harold wouldn't know the difference between an afternoon and a week.

   In Vancouver Alec skipped the conference. Instead he
walked along the ocean front, sat on chunks of driftwood,
watched the tugs worrying around the freighters. Harold
was a freighter, Alec thought, filled with his cargo of disease
and expired life. Alec was a tug. His job was to help Harold
from the stormy illusions of life, the pain of dying, into the
beautiful and serene bay of death. But Harold was resist-
ing. The dazzle beyond had no appeal. He didn't want to
be surrounded by his old friends and his old music and
pass from this vale of tears into the splendour of eternity.
For Harold death was the vale of tears, life the razzle and

the dazzle. Harold wanted to get better! He wanted life! He wanted to go to baseball games and eat hot dogs with sharp mustard.

Alec sat on the driftwood, looking out at the brave little tugs, the overburdened rusting freighters, but eventually it was only the sound of water he needed, the slow wash of the waves against the sand and rocks. He left Vancouver a day early, but when he got back to Toronto he rushed not to his brother's but to his own house. He spent the evening telling stories to Emily and Simon, then slept at peace with Margaret cuddled against him.

The next morning he took the subway north to Harold's. Harold was lying in his hospital bed, curled on one side. Francine was sponging his back. Harold's eyes swivelled towards Alec as he came into the room. They were a dark grey-green, strong and intense, and they stayed blindly fixed on Alec as he approached. Then Harold extended his hand. Alec took it. Harold's hand was cool and smooth, as though it too had been to sea, and his fingers wrapped around Alec's, taking hold.

"You have a good trip?"

"I looked at the ocean."

"Really?" Harold said, as though Alec had just announced his return from the moon.

"How are you?" Alec asked.

"Not bad," Harold said. "Then Francine's cloth hit a sore spot and Harold's fingers snapped tight while his voice broke apart, like a saw that had just run into a nail.

In August, Harold died.

Alec was left in a black vacuum. He tried to talk
himself into writing one of those books about a close one's
death that he had never been able to read. Margaret suggested he go to a psychiatrist but Alec was unable to
imagine this either. As a compromise, he didn't imagine
anything. He spent his mornings and afternoons wander-
ing about Toronto, peering at various grey activities going
on in various grey corners he hadn't looked into for a long
time. Then, at about four in the afternoon, he would start
drinking Scotch. At suppertime he'd switch to beer in
order to remain semi-conscious for the children and then,
when everyone was in bed, he'd settle down with more
Scotch and the day's obituaries. "It's a life," Alec would say
to himself, not necessarily convinced.

Alec got to the restaurant before Nancy. The postmen
were already at their post.

"Still hungry?" Nancy asked, sliding in opposite.

"Why not?" Alec said glumly.

"I was downtown last week," Nancy offered after a few
moments of silence. Nancy's trips downtown were a
running joke. She was famous for making at least one
every year.

"How was it?"

"There's a new place on Queen Street. It has this thing
where Elvis impersonators provide the music."

"Sounds perfect." That was one of Harold's expressions.

"It is."

Nancy ordered a Greek salad and Alec asked for a hot
beef sandwich, double gravy, home fries, hold the veggies.

From the restaurant they went to the office to worry about some bookkeeping problems that were causing the tax authorities to send threatening letters. Then Nancy drove him to the subway station so Alec could get to the daycare centre. On the way he looked through the obituaries of the *Sun* — a generally unploughed field for him.

Margaret was at orchestra rehearsal, so he made the children spaghetti and cheese, then he put them to bed after telling them a story to explain why his toes were crooked.

By the time Margaret got home, he was down in the basement riding his exercycle and watching an inspirational cable television show about how even the heads of large corporations would take two weeks off from their busy schedules to attend Anthony Robbins' seminars on positive thinking. On the floor around his exercycle were photocopies of articles a publisher had sent him about the woman who wades through the swamps of Borneo tracking environmentally-threatened orangutans. The publisher had suggested he write a book about this woman, but Alec was hesitating because he was unable to answer the obvious question: Why should the world's press focus on the death of a group of orangutans when thousands of people were dropping dead every minute of every day? Harold, for example. Still, he would have liked to meet this woman because he knew he'd be spending the rest of his life trying to track down Harold, convinced that in Harold's death lay the key to his own puzzle, whatever it was. No doubt she could offer him some valuable tips on extinction and survival, who went which way and why.

After his journey on the exercycle he put the photo-copied articles back in the laundry room, which was also his office, then took a shower. When he came up to the kitchen, Margaret had set out plates of cheese and fruit and a bottle of Alec's favourite Côtes du Rhone. Not for the first time he considered that Margaret was looking after him the way he had looked after Harold, suppressing her own needs and feelings to minister to his, waiting, as he had done, on the uncertain outcome, perhaps even waiting for the moment when it would be easier to hope for death than for a continuation of the pain.

He asked her opinion about the orangutan lady, watched her hesitate as though she thought this must be just a rou-tine question to be glossed over before his attention lapsed and he disconnected. As she moved on to the second glass her cheeks grew slightly flushed. He remembered how he would delight in that flush in the old days, watch for it as though it were a rare but perfect twilight that guaranteed smooth sailing into the darkest of nights.

Eventually the wine, or perhaps Alec had also been helped by the inspirational business program, sent them upstairs. Then Alec lost the thread and found himself won-dering what Harold might think of the fact that only months after his death Alec was drinking his favourite wine and making love. He decided Harold would approve — he'd always liked a party — but the whole idea made Alec afraid that if he didn't pay attention their flesh might fall away from their bones and their skeletons start clacking.

When Alec wrote his article about "Herbert Franz Strauss Meyser and The European Male", he ended it

with his own theory: that the next step in cultural evolution would be electronic brains to travel the electronic
highway everyone was always boasting about these days,
and that people would simply be there to manufacture
and serve them. Writing this article, sometimes late at
night while watching Harold sleep, he had not spent five
seconds worrying about the fact that he was predicting the
enslavement, or possibly even the end of, the entire human
race. Extinction, evolution, mass disaster — somehow they
had all been replaced by his obsession with the dying and
death of just one person.

"You've read all the big books," Harold challenged him
one day near the end. "What does it all mean?"

"I don't know," Alec said. Ever since his return from
Vancouver, he'd been desperately hoping Harold would
make some sort of announcement that would indicate he
was reconciled to his own death. But of course he wasn't.
He was still furious that he was dying; he felt robbed of
life, cheated for no reason. Alec also felt Harold was being
robbed and cheated — but against all reason and un-
reason Harold *was* dying. Harold also currently believed
he was living in a dresser drawer too short for him and that
meteorites had crashed through the roof of the house,
causing this emergency situation. He locked his long
fingers around Alec's hand.

"I don't know anything," Harold then said, and his
fingers relaxed. Sometimes Alec would stand beside
Harold's bed and massage his shoulders, his back, while
Harold, temporarily rescued by morphine, managed to
drift away for a while. Then Alec would feel the way he

had as a child when Harold, barely more than a baby, would come to him in pain and Alec, sitting silently beside him, holding his hand or rubbing his back, would draw the pain away until nothing was left except the strange unknown outside world, and the little club they had formed to protect themselves against it. "How long do you want me to keep going?" Alec would ask, his muscles sore from massaging Harold.

"As long as you can take it."

Near the end Harold lay blind in a bed from which he hadn't moved for weeks. The hair on his head, his eyebrows, his moustache had grown back. But his fingers had remained permanently transformed to their guitar-playing selves.

"I've been lying here for months, you know what I mean? I've gone over all the details."

"I know," Alec said.

"It all adds up to nothing, *nada, rien.* That's my final word on the subject." Silence. "So that's it. I don't have any speeches. Do you have any speeches? You were always good at making speeches."

"You won the public speaking contest," Alec said.

"I don't have any speeches now. Maybe later. What about you? Are you going to make a speech?"

"I'm just putting it together."

"Good. Work on it. I'm not going anywhere."

Clean day, clean start. A cold November rain spattered against the windows. Alec closed his eyes, stumbled. It was as though an invisible stranger had bumped into him.

Again he saw himself standing at his brother's grave. The
bright August sun. The perfect summer breeze. The over-
fertilized geraniums sparkling brightly from the other
graves. His brother's closed coffin. The way it had jolted
into the ground while all the uncles and nabobs of the
synagogue whispered their disapproval. The sound of
stone-filled earth rattling against the coffin. A lifetime
before, Alec had stood with Harold only a few steps away,
watching his father's casket receiving its blanket of stony
earth. That time Alec had himself helped to cover the
coffin. Seventy years, three score years and ten, his father
had lived — a self-declared agnostic who nonetheless
regarded himself as straight out of the Bible and was determined to extract from life his biblical due. He had died
suddenly in the bathroom after dinner, while his wife was
preparing him a cup of decaffeinated coffee, skim milk,
one sugar. Ripe with unquestioned pride in his sons, and
full of what he considered the essential doctrine for a successful life: the conviction that, as he frequently put it,
"my shit smells better". After the funeral Alec and Harold
left the relatives at the house and went to buy more liquor
for the reception and shiva.

Dressed in their suits, they had stood for a few
moments in the liquor store parking lot. This was, after all,
an unusual occasion. That they would both be dressed in
suits. That they would be looking at each other, white
shirt to white shirt, tie to tie. That it would all be happening in the parking lot of a liquor store — a place, Alec
couldn't help thinking, that would be a lot better suited to
funerals than was the Jewish cemetery with its uniform

tombstones, its obligatory geraniums, its part-time Jews clutching yarmulkas to their heads every time a breeze blew up.

Harold had pulled out his cigarettes. "Here we are," Alec said, "standing in the liquor store parking lot getting cancer after our father's funeral."

They were beside a suburban-style pickup truck with a load of cedar fence posts. Then in came a big lime-green, swoop-finned Chevrolet with tail-lights studded like the fake ruby cufflinks Alec had worn for his bar mitzvah, the bass of its sound system pounding into the pavement while Elvis screamed out "Jailhouse Rock".

"Perfect," Harold said.

The sound switched off as the door opened and the driver, a woman, jumped out and came straight towards Harold. "Sorry to hear about your father," she said. Harold stood loosely, one shoulder a bit forward, smiling and nodding. He mumbled an introduction. Alec watched the woman relax; like many women around Harold, she seemed to bask in his presence, as though his aura were a hot tub she was eager to try.

"Really," she said. "I am sorry," She put her hand on Harold's arm, stood on her toes to kiss him, then gave Alec a quick nod and moved off.

"Another member of the fan club?"

"I wish," Harold said, and then started towards the store.

The day after Harold's funeral Alec woke at dawn and slipped out of the house to walk. He came to a street where he and Harold had once shared a joint on the way to eat dinner at a neighbourhood restaurant.

"Great stuff," Harold had said, pulling it out of the suit coat he'd worn to meet a client. "Do you ever wonder why everyone else has stopped?"

"Not everyone," Alec had assured him. In the restaurant Harold charmed the waitress by speaking the elegant French he'd learned in about five minutes, the way he learned everything.

Alec stopped to look in the restaurant window. A grey light filled the room. All the chairs were upside down on the tables and in the corner a mop was angled into a plastic bucket. Alec couldn't imagine himself with Harold, couldn't feel Harold's presence. At least nothing benevolent. Nothing more than the faint echo of a desperate terrified cry he wanted to think he was imagining. Or maybe the cry was real but coming not from Harold but himself. The timid beginnings of his grief. At the loss. At the way he'd failed Harold.

"I'm counting on you. You're not going to leave me, are you?" Late at night. Overflowing with pain. Harold's moans and cries floating through the open windows and into the street, drowning out the traffic, the sounds of children playing softball, birds, breeze, chipmunks — the whole list.

Alec looked in the restaurant window and instead of seeing Harold and himself sitting there, eating imitation steak and frites and testing their French on a waitress who deserved better, he saw Harold in the liquor store parking lot, his cigarette balanced between two long fingers, eyes slowly turning towards the swoop-finned Chevrolet. Harold as a child running with his arms outstretched. Harold standing beside a barbecue, beer in hand, slapping marinated meat onto the sizzling grill, great clouds of smoke drifting up into air already filled by sweet electric sound, urgent chatter and sharp barks of laughter.

Harold's utter shock when anything went wrong. "Oh, *Jesus*." The way his face would crumple. The betrayal of it all. The incredible unwanted fact that the universe, this warm friendly rock-and-roll heaven where everything was beautiful and easy, could suddenly turn and tear at him like some kind of deranged snake. Never for very long, of course, except for the last time which was for ever.

Mid-afternoon. Queen Street. Alec was standing beside a stalled streetcar. Its wires were down; heads poked out of windows while the conductor and two cops tried to set things right. The drivers in the backed-up cars leaned on their horns.

It was overcast; thick, dark clouds were being pushed along by a cold wind. Alec heard a voice calling what he thought was his name across the traffic. He looked up. Across the street, between a discount electronics shop and a second-hand bookstore was the sign: a vertical rectangle with CLUB ELVIS in red letters surrounded by lime-green vines against a yellow background that looked faded and indecisive, as though it had been there for years.

The CLUB ELVIS sign hung above a narrow passageway that led to a door in a small courtyard. Alec stopped. Officially he was on his way to the bookstore to find Simon some books on evolution that he remembered reading as a child. His favourite had been *How Man Became A Giant* because the fur-skirted caveman on the cover — who was standing on top of a woolly mammoth and waving his spear in triumph — used to remind him of his father on his way to shave.

Now Alec remembered that Nancy had mentioned this Club Elvis place. He looked at his watch. Four o'clock. Two hours until the daycare closed. He hesitated. Through a break in the noise from the street he heard a smooth rum-soaked voice crooning to the soft strains of a Hawaiian guitar.

The song twanged to an end as he came in the door. On stage was a huge transvestite Elvis, his beard shadow looming through his camellia white make-up like a cloud waiting to burst over a picnic. He was wearing a dark red velvet dress that revealed a glistening white chest; his thick greasy black hair coiled down to his shoulders.

"This is a special number the Colonel always liked," the deep voice drawled in a tone so smoothly oiled, so hypnotically sepulchral, that Alec sat down at a table near the back. Then he/she began singing "Love Me Tender". Lush chords issued from his/her guitar, a chorus swelled up to join them. "Sing it, Nymphets," encouraged the Elvis, and the spotlights fell on four women dressed in maroon jogging clothes.

A waiter passed by with a tray of draft beer. By the time Alec had reached into his pocket and paid, a new Elvis — a lanky wide-jawed man with a ducktail whose wings looked like they had been caught in an oil spill — had taken the stage and was doing a spaghetti-legged dance with a golden teddy bear he was clutching to his chest.

Now a group of men sitting near the front stood up. Alec saw they were all wearing red sweaters, as though they were from the same office. They shuffled to the foot of the stage, made a straggly line with their arms over each other's shoulders, and began to do a slow beery kick-dance.

Alec looked around the club. At one side the "Nymphets" were sitting at a big table, drinking cocktails and chatting. Maybe they were the female side of the office. At a table along the opposite wall was a couple leaning so close their heads touched. Alec remembered how when he started going out with Margaret they would sneak off to empty restaurants and taverns, spend hours looking into each other's eyes, hold hands, let their legs slide together as though by coincidence.

The music stopped but the men were still dancing. One of them, Alec now noticed, looked a bit like Harold. At least he had the full, wide moustache Harold used to have, and when he grinned the smile flashed a familiar wink.

The same thing had happened to Alec after his father's death: he kept seeing men just like him — old geezers in car coats wearing polyester pants cut too short, with over-sized faces and thin black hair combed straight back, dark plastic glasses that made marks on their big immigrant noses. They would usually be wearing plaid somewhere. Alec would catch up to them, walk beside them for a few seconds, peer right into their faces trying desperately to remember some mole or mark that would distinguish his father from these strangers. Then the bubble would burst and Alec would move on. Some of these imitation fathers would look out at him from a car window. Or be glimpsed crossing a street or in a movie as the lights went down. When he confessed this to Harold, Harold laughed and said, "Oh sure, I see him fifty times a week. There must be a million of them out there. Ghost Dads."

By now the man in the chorus line seemed to have noticed Alec. Alec began to feel very nervous. He was going to have to get right next to him, the way he had to his father's imitators.

He picked up his beer and moved to a table in front of the stage. The man stopped dancing and spoke directly to Alec. "You're staring at me," he said, not unpleasantly. His voice, too, reminded Alec of Harold: low, thickly textured, shaded by a drawl that stretched out when he'd had a few drinks.

"Excuse me," Alec said, "I couldn't help myself. You look exactly like my brother."

The man sat down. Then he leaned forward. His fingers. The hair on his knuckles. The vitality that radiated out of him the way oranges smell of orange or light comes from the sun. "Is there anything about your brother I should know?"

"He's dead," Alec said. "Don't take it personally."

"Okay," said the man in his Harold-like voice. "Why don't we have a beer and think about it?"

Why don't we have a beer and think about it! This was so "Harold" it could pass for his motto. Not that Harold drank much beer. He loved to have a beer in his hand, but actually drinking it was a lot less interesting.

Other Elvises came on stage. The Nymphets accompanied them to recorded soundtracks. Alec sat, entranced, smiling at this stranger who was toying with his beer, smiling back.

Alec began to worry about getting to the daycare. It was his turn to pick up the children, but he couldn't take his eyes off the stranger to look at his watch. For the first time since Harold's death the world felt whole again. He took a deep breath. It was *centuries* since he had breathed a breath like this. He took another. His belly grew content and round, like that of a happy Buddha glowing with peaceful satisfaction.

Finally Alec said, "I've got to make a phone call but I'm afraid to."

"Why?"

"I'm afraid you'll leave while I'm gone."

"I won't. I promise."

Alec looked across the room. There was a telephone on the bar. "Just a second," he said, then backed away from the table, keeping his eyes on this man who looked and sounded like his dead brother. Still watching him he called Margaret and explained that he'd gone for a walk, started thinking about Harold and gone into a bar. Now he was so drunk he didn't want the children to see him — could she pick them up? In that understanding voice she had concerning all aspects of Harold's death, a voice which apparently released him from all normal obligations due to this unprecedented emergency, Margaret told Alec to relax, come home when he was ready.

When he got back to the table the stranger held out the palm of his hand, the way Harold used to, then opened his mouth to talk. The shape of his tongue, the exact way his lips slid up over his teeth. Alec couldn't stop staring. *My eyes are popping out of my head*, Alec thought. *My eyes and my ears.* Because a loud internal alarm was filling his skull as he took in the stranger's soft green eyes, the slow curve of his nose, the stubby bristles of his moustache. Suddenly he was so frightened he opened his mouth to scream. It was Harold.

"You!" Alec said. "Why didn't you call me or something?"

"I was going to. And then, well — here you are." Harold signalled to the waiter.

The transvestite was back on stage singing "Rock Around The Clock". The after-work crowd was starting to drift in. A few musicians had appeared on stage and were setting up.

"I don't even know what to ask," Alec said.

"Just enjoy it." Harold had taken out some cigarettes; now he opened the pack, put one in front of Alec before helping himself. He leaned forward to give Alec a light and Alec noticed he was using the cylindrical gold lighter he used to have.

The club filled up and the sounds of talk and laughter made their own tidal waves while, on stage, the imitation Elvises re-lived the history of rock and roll. Platters of chicken wings arrived, charred and covered in a dark pungent sauce. Coloured spots began to play over the stage and audience. Harold's face took on a deep red glow. Every time Alec looked down, a new glass of beer was standing beside his hand. He would lift it, drink from it, wash away the questions. So many questions. But what was there to ask? Harold had definitely died. First, Alec had watched him waste away for several months. Second, he had sat in the room with him when he was dead. Third, he had watched him being carried out of the house.

Harold began quizzing Alec about Margaret, the children, his work. Harold had fallen sick before Alec had had a chance to tell him how his article on Dr. Meyser was progressing and that the article, with Alec's crazy theory about electronic brains, had led to a book commission on "The Death of European Culture". If nothing else, it would at least impress the university with the idea he must be doing *something*. Now, with Harold, a conversation about the future of mankind seemed more ridiculous than ever. But every time Alec tried to turn the questions back, or even to talk about Nancy instead of Margaret, the music would start up and Harold would look away, or he would get that expression on his face that meant he didn't want to discuss it, whatever *it* was. "We'll get to that later," he said a couple of times, easily. Then, when Alec pushed once more: "Tonight let's talk about you. Tomorrow it can be my turn."

Alec was reassured. At least there would be a tomorrow.

"Of course. I'll be right here," Harold said when the lights came up and Alec realized he was one of the last customers. "Drop around in the afternoon, like today. Any time. No one's going anywhere. I promise."

As Alec walked out and towards Queen Street he looked back at the club. Harold was standing in the doorway, one hand in his pocket, leaning jauntily, his free arm held high — waving.

4

Alec stood in his own front hall. Upstairs was dark except for the faint glow of the bathroom night-light. He took off his shoes.

From the moment he left Club Elvis he'd had the strange feeling that somehow, with Harold, he had entered the kingdom of the dead. The voices of passers-by were garbled and in a language he no longer understood, their faces white and congealed. Since Harold's death everything and everyone had existed at an uncrossable remove. Except for his children. They alone had travelled with him into the no-world he now occupied — cheerful, oblivious, determined that he continue both to give and to receive.

Now, standing at the foot of the stairs, he could hear his children breathing. Simon slept with a deep rasping breath. Emily's breath was a little silken whisper he'd often knelt and listened to, nights he'd come home from Harold's dying. Margaret was the one who slept silently. Silent, immobile, her sleeps were like deep trances during which she abandoned her body. Nothing woke her but unpredictable nightmares from which she'd emerge shouting "What?" or "Help!"

On these occasions Alec — who seemed to himself never really to sleep but rather to spend the night twisting in bed, bobbing in and out of consciousness — would reply: "I was just talking about the furnace," or "Everything's under control," or "Emily was just packing her lunch."

Tonight Alec was glad to see the light out in their bedroom, to know Margaret was lost in a sleep he could not disturb. To know he would not yet have to explain what had happened. In his stocking feet he walked down the hall to the kitchen. The microwave read 2:36. He sat down in the dark. The refrigerator motor was making its eternal buzz, the neighbour's heat pump was in labour, and in whatever space was left he could hear the bass thumping from the late-night practice of the band who lived on the next block.

He opened the kitchen window. Along with a rush of cold damp air, the music came in more loudly. He looked into the refrigerator: quarts of milk and orange juice stood like icons in the white light. As he reached for the juice the light hit his own hand, turning the flesh as chalky as the forehead of the transvestite Elvis. The veins on the back of his hands seemed suddenly thick and ropy. His heart made a little sputter. He froze for a moment. JOURNALIST SUFFERS SUDDEN HEART ATTACK WHILE STANDING IN FRONT OF REFRIGERATOR. He imagined Simon hearing him slump to the floor. Simon, marked by the curse of the eldest, would be the first to register that one heart less was beating, the first to leap out of bed, rush downstairs, find his father lying dead in the white refrigerator light with a jar of horseradish in his hand because he'd picked it up to check its date, Simon would guess, Alec having trained him in obsessively checking the expiry date of everything from muffins to apple juice.

While he waited to see if he was having a heart attack, Alec managed to verify that the horseradish still had a few months left, slide it back into place and close the door, so Simon could at least find him in the dark and be spared the shock of discovering him in a pool of artificial light.

More time passed. Alec closed the kitchen window. From the bedroom directly above, he heard the bed creaking, Margaret's footsteps leading to the bathroom. Alec froze. He realized he was soaked in sweat. Now she was coming down the stairs. The microwave said 2:42. At the foot of the stairs she looked into the kitchen. Through the window of the front door shone a streetlight, turning the fuzzy edges of Margaret's hair into a pale halo. She was peering into the darkness, right at him, but of course she couldn't see him. Either because it was too dark, or because, led by Harold, he had crossed into the kingdom of the dead and could no longer be seen by the living. Nonetheless, if she came any closer he would have to stand up, switch on the light, explain himself.

She turned around and went upstairs.

As Margaret's footsteps made a new trail to the bedroom, Alec began his quiet pilgrimage to the foot of the stairs. There, crouched in the shadows, he listened to Margaret as she slid her feet between the sheets, turned with a light grunt and pulled the pillow into position.

The peace he'd arrived at with Harold had entirely disappeared. Instead he had become an uneasy witness to the glow of his family's mutual love, the protective web his wife and children had spun in his absence, a web he was outside of. Margaret's breathing fell into the silence of her sleep. Looking upstairs to his bedroom, the rectangle of the door-frame a dim silhouette from the bathroom night-light, he saw the room begin to move, the ship of his family gradually sailing away from him into the future.

He wondered if this was how it would be if he died, then came back to haunt the house. If standing in the front hall he would feel this terrible ripping in his chest as he, dead, mourned to the sound of his family leaving him behind.

As he tiptoed into Simon's room, Simon, who always slept on his back, flung out one of his arms. His face was smooth and angelic. His long lashes curled into shadows, his lips were slightly parted. When Simon had been a baby, his crib in this room, Alec had often come to soothe him when he cried in the night. Sometimes he would sit in the armchair at the foot of the crib, hold Simon in his arms and, rocking him back and forth, tell him stories about things he and Harold had done as children. In these stories — more lies than truth — he recounted their adventures: how they'd paddled their canoe through the wilderness; the terrible cold they'd endured waiting for buses; the funny feeling he'd had the day he pushed Harold down the stairs; the strange scum left in the toilet after you tried to flush down fish fingers and scalloped potatoes.

Of course Simon had understood none of this — he was only six months old. But that didn't matter. Simon was getting shaped and branded, the same way Alec's father had shaped and branded Alec. Alec couldn't remember how it had happened, only that after a certain point he could feel his father inside him, inhabiting him. Like when he walked a certain way, turning one foot out more than the other — and he could jump outside himself and see his father shuffling along with that exact-same strange half-hitched gait that made it seem, some days, he was about to break into a dance, or, on others, that he was going to fall on his face.

If he lived long enough, Alec knew, he would end up with that strange dance/stumble. Until it was Simon's turn. Smooth angelic Simon with the dark reddish curls, the supple boy's body that loved to fling itself across the ice in front of a hockey net. Acrobatic Simon who loved to turn and twist in mid-air, the way Alec once had turned and twisted.

Alec was crying noisily. Simon's eyes opened, but like Margaret's they seemed to stare right through him. "It's all right," Alec said. He took his son's hand in his; Simon's eyes closed and he drifted back into his dream.

Emily's room was darker. He had to put his face right against hers to see her. And when he did, she wrapped her arms around his neck, holding their faces together — the way she used to when she was a baby and could sucker Alec into bringing her into their bed.

Alec kissed Emily's nose. Her nose, her mouth, her whole face smelled of cinnamon chewing gum. He unwrapped her arms, then sat on the floor beside her bed.

Emily's breathing. Simon's breathing. Margaret's silence.

Slowly he crawled into the hall and towards his bedroom. Whenever the floor creaked he stopped, redistributed his weight, then carefully began again. Finally he was kneeling beside his bed. Margaret's back was to him, her knees drawn up to her chest. There was something so trusting about the way Margaret slept — her back to him, the door, the hall, the children, the whole house. And yet, unlike the children, he couldn't simply reach and touch her without waking her. Couldn't press his face against hers, then leave her asleep. Couldn't, for her, cross the blackness that had surrounded him ever since Harold died.

He took off his clothes and got into bed. He lay on his back, his leg along Margaret. She shifted to adjust to him, curled a foot around one of his insteps.

One morning six months ago, when he was sitting at Harold's bedside and reading him spring training reports from the newspaper, Harold had whispered, *Shhhh.* Between them that had always been an inviolable call for silence, a warning that a parent was about to discover them in some illegal activity. *Shhhh,* Harold had whispered again, raising a long finger. Then his eyebrows went up and the comically huge whites of his eyes rolled towards the ceiling.

"What profiteth a man if he earn his living but lose his soul?" Harold asked.

Alec put down the paper and tried to think of an answer. "Well?"

"I don't know," Alec said.

"Could you find out?" Harold asked, his voice suddenly the plaintive one he used to request a cup of decaf or assistance to the bathroom.

"Well?" Harold had demanded again later that day and Alec, who kept hoping Harold would somehow arrive at that point of balance which would allow him to endure, could only come up with: "You could use the money to buy a decent sound system."

"Oh, my older brother is *so funny*," Harold said in a bitter voice that made Alec's stomach feel as though a sword were passing through it. And though he looked at Harold's face for some sign of softening or forgiveness, none was there. His face was twisted into just a single expression, an ideogram with one idea: I am dying; you are making fun of me because you are not up to it. And Alec knew Harold was at least half right — he wasn't up to Harold's dying. Though he endlessly conducted with himself all the conversations Harold refused to have, he had no real answers to Harold's real question: Why him? Like Harold, his only answer to every other question had always been *life*: wild dancing, sex, love, music, drugs, babies, food.

Margaret groaned and turned in her sleep, putting her head against Alec's shoulder and throwing her arm across his chest. In spite of everything, Alec slept.

The next afternoon Alec found his way back to Club Elvis. When he went in the place was utterly dark, except for a tiny spot shining on an empty stage. Alec groped forward and felt for a chair.

There was a drum roll, a few lush chords. As the lights came up Alec could see the transvestite Elvis standing at the microphone. But today he was dressed as a man,

tightly encased in studded black leather that bulged
obscenely as he leered and wriggled his hips. Alec shiv-
ered. Harold was sitting across from him. He wasn't laughing aloud but he had on his new post-mortal, big-easy
smile, a big shit-eating white-toothed grin that lit up his
mouth under his wide moustache.

"Laugh, Alec." Harold's hand flicked out, touched
Alec's shoulder. Harold's fingers were hot. Alec felt, literally, jolted. A blaze of electric current spread around the
outside of his body. Looking down he could see he was
wrapped in a translucent shell swept by clouds of sheet
lightning. Then Harold snapped his fingers and the shell
exploded. Alec laughed. He could feel the laugh sucking
air deep into his belly, running up through his lungs and
then flowing out his throat, a smooth purring chuckle that
made his whole body glow.

"How's that?" Harold asked.

"Great."

Now Alec saw that there was a third person at the table.
Francine. He hadn't seen Francine since Harold's funeral,
where she had been a golden angel draped in black, unap-
proachable and armoured in her grief, the bitter twist of
her mouth. Afterwards there had been drinks — a gathering of the faithful at Harold's house — but Francine had
not appeared. Now the mourning garments had given way
to cowboy vest and embroidered shirt, her sun-bright hair
cascaded to her shoulders, and as she leaned towards Alec
and put her hand on his sleeve, her eyes were shining in
triumph.

"Hello," she said. "Welcome to the club. How have you been? And how did you find us?"

"Well," Alec said, "it was almost a coincidence."

When Francine laughed Harold made a sound to go along with her and Alec felt that smooth purring chuckle flowing through him again, a gilded Rolls Royce of happiness that sank through his belly to his groin and kept going until his toes began to wiggle with it.

Up on stage Elvis was moving into "Love Me Tender", and as he sang and danced the coils of his black hair snaked around his neck and shoulders. The male chorus line, arms about each other's waists, swayed back and forth. They were wearing straw hats and Hawaiian leis, and all of them were smiling. On the other side of Elvis, the Nymphets hummed heavenly accords. Alec wondered if they were also members of the club, if every hum and chuckle made their bodies feel like a nuclear power station melting down into satori.

"Let's go," Harold said. He stood up and beckoned with his head.

They went through a door Alec hadn't noticed, then filed down a dark narrow corridor. There was a small set of stairs, another corridor, then suddenly they were out in the parking lot.

"Here we are," Harold said, then climbed into the driver's seat of a canvas-topped Range Rover. Soon they were driving across centre town. When they got to the beach, Harold stopped. It was cold. Alec was wearing an old leather bomber jacket with a fur collar. Over his red sweater Harold had put on a suit jacket but, like Francine who wore no coat at all, he seemed immune to the icy wind coming off the water.

"This is the idea," Harold said, pulling his black attaché case and three lawn chairs out of the back: "We sit here all night drinking, then we watch the sun come up."

They unfolded the chairs. The attaché case had its usual consignment of grappa, along with three glasses. Soon they were on a second drink, then a third. Gradually Alec became immersed in the sound of lapping waves, the cries of gulls and sandpipers.

Alec dozed off. He woke up. There was more grappa. The pitch darkness turned into a long arc of horizon with a glimmering ribbon of light. The birds. The water. The breeze rasping through the few remaining leaves.

"Well? Is this perfect or what?"

Alec turned towards his brother. Something happened in Harold's face, a sudden pale flicker, a draining, a little hiccup in time. Unable to stop himself Alec reached out. But it was too late. Harold had died again and was now slumped in his chair, his head tilted to one side and his own arm extended, as though to meet Alec's hand. There was a slight smile on his face, his moon-white skin filled with light.

Alec was kneeling by his brother's chair when he felt Francine's hand on his shoulder. Soft, hesitant.

"What's going on?" Harold was rubbing his face the way he used to when he woke up after a deep sleep. "Sorry," he said. "These late nights."

Meanwhile the sun had risen and a pale yellow light was sweeping across the beach. Off to the side was a catering truck. Joggers and early morning dog-walkers were standing around, drinking coffee and chatting.

"That looks good," Harold said.

"I'll go," Alec volunteered. At the truck he got three lidded cups of coffee along with a supply of cream containers and sugar. Walking back he was facing directly into the sun. When he closed his eyes, yellow-white shards of light jangled in his skull. He had a throbbing headache and his eyes felt the way they had one afternoon after he and Harold had gone cross-country skiing at the cabin and ended up with snow blindness for two days, the white-snow light exploding in their brains while they stumbled about the cabin feeding the stove and waiting to see again.

When Alec opened his eyes he couldn't find Harold, Francine or the chairs. Then he picked out two figures strolling along the water. As he ran towards them the lids came loose from the cups and scalding coffee spilled onto his hands and wrists. But it turned out the people he'd spotted were strangers.

Alec began jogging north across the beach, towards the boardwalk and into the park. Nothing. He found the place where the Range Rover had been parked but it too had disappeared.

O NE day soon Herr Meyser and I will take a walk. It will be spring and I'll be at the cabin again. In the woods the remaining snow will be wet and crystalline between the trees. I'll kneel to smell the bright green moss. Roll over on my back and look up at soft spring clouds through the leafless branches of the silver maples. The clouds will push across the sky, powered by the southwest wind that always blows on those first spring days, carrying raw warm air across the melting fields, pushing the ducks and geese northward, sending last year's chipmunks scurrying along wet icy ridges, twisting in the trees like tiny monkeys, doing their spring chipmunk tricks to the songs of woodpeckers and grosbeaks, crows calling for carrion, the high-pitched cries of marsh hawks circling the damp grass.

Herr Meyser is Harold's hat. He used to live in a box stored on a shelf of Harold's coat closet, ready for special occasions. In those golden days Herr Meyser's felt was a uniform pearly grey, his brim flat, his crown perfectly shaped, his satin lining unstained by sweat or grease.

Those were Herr Meyser's salad days, the days when he could have been the crowning glory of a morning suit, a cashmere coat, a body-shaven weightlifter wearing only Herr Meyser and knee-garters.

Harold and I once had knee-garters. We were in the fifty-first scout troop, a Hebrew school unit faithful to the queen and Lord Baden-Powell, although the hot dogs and steaks we grilled on our overnight camping trips had to be guaranteed kosher, and when we played dodgeball in the synagogue basement we were forbidden to use prayer books as shields.

My scouting career went into a decline when, after a few months, I actually read *Scouting for Boys*, a manual by Lord Baden-Powell that placed a suspicious emphasis on frequent cold showers followed by "brisk rub-downs with rough towels". What exactly was he getting at? I resigned immediately, explaining to the troop leader that I was leaving the scouting movement in order to devote myself to violin lessons.

Harold persisted for another year. He had two pairs of garters. They were black elastic numbers that went around the calf and were meant to hold up the scratchy green stockings that matched the green handkerchiefs we wore around our necks. A picture still exists of us in our scout uniforms; we have dimples and are saluting the camera. We look pitiful.

Herr Meyser was the hat Harold wore after chemotherapy took away his hair, and I put on Herr Meyser for Harold's funeral. Herr Meyser's grey was not a perfect

match for my dark blue suit, the same one I wore for my
father's funeral and which required either a black hat or a
yarmulka, but loyalty dictated my choice. Although he still
lived in his box, Herr Meyser's brim had gained a few
water spots and was starting to curl at the edges. Harold's
head was also bigger than mine, which meant that
between the over-large crown and wide brim, I was sufficiently hidden to be able to cry in private. As is the
custom, Harold's coffin — closed — was at the front of the
synagogue. His body had been washed and ritually prepared. Harold's body was not something I wanted to think
about but, with the coffin in front of me, such thoughts
were impossible to avoid. So I thought about Harold's
body. Not much changed, I supposed, from the last time I
had seen it, which was the day before, half an hour after
he died. At that point his body was thin and shrunken, his
face serene, his skin, as they say, a deathly white. His long
fingers were still supple, his moustache and fingernails
still growing. With his grey growing moustache and his
large skull fringed by grey hair at his temples, he looked,
under his white sheet, like a Roman senator. A noble
Roman senator struck down by all that was not noble. Yet
finally, after everything that had happened, he also looked
reconciled to his fate. Of course I needed to believe that.

    Shortly after the funeral I came up to the cabin,
looking to console myself or maybe just to get connected
to the ground that was connected to Harold. I brought
Herr Meyser with me, not his first visit, since he'd already
accompanied Harold. I can see Harold and me sitting on

a small hummock above the cabin, my favourite place to watch the sun set over the woodshed. There's a shallow pit surrounded by a circle of stones, and in the pit, in the darkening twilight, glowing embers match the red-stained sky and barred clouds. Herr Meyser sits on Harold's head, soaking up the smoke. There's the staccato crackling of poplar leaves in the light breeze. The loud slow plod of a porcupine sneaking around the cabin to the blackberry bushes on the far side of the tile bed. Red-winged black-birds singing from the marsh down by the road. Harold's face hidden as he stirs the embers with a piece of sumac.

Some part of me is enchanted by this. The setting suns, the walks in the fields, nights marked by fire and birds, the cries of unknown animals as they kill and make love in the darkness, the beavers beavering across the pond, the swoop of bats and the pointed staring faces of raccoons. Harold knew that world and travelled through it, but where I was enchanted, he was finally bored. Harold needed something else, something to do with the cellular telephone he carried in the trunk of his car, the black attaché case filled with magic and grappa, the bank balances that didn't balance, the gremlins in his nervous system that kept his toes tapping, his fingers snapping, his eyes nervously moving. Harold needed the hunt. Harold needed to be a secret agent in the pay of an unknown power, to be wearing tinted glasses and a trenchcoat and be twirling Herr Meyser on the tip of a long finger as he winked at the camera at the conclusion of another thrilling and hilarious episode of *Harold's Greatest Cases*.

2

Memory. The way it enfolds and protects. Protects and conceals. Like a fist. My father's hands, wide muscular palms shaped by the handle of the sledgehammer he used for breaking the copper out of batteries in *his* father's junk-yard. Those were the days. In family photographs, a row of children stand stiffly between a bearded patriarch wearing suspenders over his white shirt and my grandmother in her ubiquitous black dress. My father's face is frozen with fear, his big hands pinned awkwardly to his sides, fingers helpless to stop flexing. My father's face is scarlet with anger, his big hand sweeping towards me. I am unmoving. A deer transfixed by the headlights. His red face is at an angle, his glasses jiggle on his nose, his hair, still black and thick then, flies out with the violence that has taken hold of him, that primitive god of violence and domination that has set him upon his first son.

When the hand arrives I howl in pain and outrage. My father's temper. My father's rages. My father's shame. The battles of wills he can't win — against himself, against me, against my mother. The battles he can't win but can't give up because he is the most stubborn.

Then Harold is born. Harold likes to hold my hand and follow me around. Harold is smaller, he can't hurt me. Though sometimes I hurt Harold. When he is most vulnerable and least expects it. Until eventually Harold hurts me. When I am most vulnerable and least expect it.

Time passes. Things happen. I go to university. Harold leaves home.

One day my father bumped his head on a car door. It gave him double vision. When it wouldn't go away he went to see his doctor. A few weeks later he was sitting on the edge of a downtown Toronto hospital bed, waiting to get his breastbone sawn open so his thymus gland could be removed. I was visiting him. The father I had feared, the red-faced giant who had frozen me in the white light of his rage, had disappeared. Now my father had a wide generous face, an elephant-eared, big-nosed, large-jawed face that made everyone feel so comfortable they teased him about it. The temper had burned out or gone into hiding or gotten knocked to pieces on the golf course.

He was drinking Scotch out of a flask. He explained to me that when he had proposed to my mother she had made him promise to live until he was at least seventy years old. Since he was more than fifteen years older than her, she needed a guarantee he would survive until the children she wanted to have with him were grown. That day in the hospital, the day he was drinking Scotch while waiting to have his chest sawn open, my father still owed my mother four years. Being a man of his word he intended, he explained, to survive without making a fuss. Saying this, his face firmed into concrete. I got the message: he was walking naked into enemy fire and he expected to be torn to shreds. For reasons he couldn't explain and possibly didn't know, he was expected to endure this.

The next week, after the surgery, Harold and I went to visit him. Our father was looking a lot worse. Connected to machines, breathing with the aid of a respirator, his myopic eyes were fixed on the ceiling, his hands alternately gripping the blanket and flexing. Drinking Scotch out of flasks was not an option. I put my hands over his. "Breathe with me," I said. As we breathed I squeezed his hands slowly, trying to will him into painlessness, serenity, the little chamber of eternity I still believed each of us could walk into like a long-neglected room. Harold's face was crumpled. When my mother came to relieve us, we went back to my place and drank the Scotch my father could not.

Appropriately enough, we drank out of glasses my father had given me as a house-warming present. The glasses were short and stubby, but capacious. As we drank I remembered how, on the afternoon my father had come to inspect and give his blessing, he had sat opposite me in the very chair Harold now occupied. My father's wide smile, his wide hand surrounding the thick-cut glass, moving it slowly back and forth, making ice music in the summer heat.

At that time I was starting graduate school and Harold was working at an advertising agency owned by a family friend famous for his heavy drinking and his locker-room limericks. Released from the chains of compulsory educa-tion, Harold became an overnight success and a total opti-mist: the world was on the highway to a better future and he was firmly in the driver's seat, making a salary so high he didn't dare reveal it to my parents. I was the serious one, the studious older brother carefully combing through mankind's most important ideas in search of something that might prevent the next holocaust or get rid of television. As my father drank with me he was toasting not only my first apartment, but his hope that his eldest son would spend the rest of his life with his nose in a book, advancing the human enterprise. "You and Harold are just the same," I wanted to tell him. "Optimists." I was proudly opposite, a flag-waving nihilist. In my sage opinion everything was going straight downhill and I didn't find it depressing at all; on the contrary, I thought that of all directions downhill was the most exciting, as in downhill skiing. I was about to explain this to my father when he said, "You know, sometimes I worry about Harold."

"He's coining it," I said, using one of Harold's favourite expressions.

"Coining it?"

"Making piles of money. Doing incredibly well."

"Lenny says that too. It was nice of him to take Harold on at the agency."

"It's not a favour. Harold's really good."

"What does he do, exactly?"

"Has ideas, I guess."

My father set his glass down, satisfied. He nodded his head contentedly. "I thought so," he said. He looked down at his hands as though to make sure they'd absorbed this new information.

On that day my father shook my hand at the door of my new apartment, walked slowly down the stairs. I stood at the window, watching him get into his car. My father was feeling, I knew, the satisfaction he experienced when looking at a lawn he had mowed, a scientific paper he had published. Another victory to be chalked up to the empire of reason and the passage of time. I, meanwhile, was boiling with anger. My father was driving down the street, happy to have shared a drink with his eldest son, but his eldest son couldn't forget the red-faced giant he might possibly have invented. The scornful twist of the giant's mouth when the son deserted the neatly ploughed fields of science for the useless and unfaithful world of arts and letters. The cold silence as he listened to haltingly expressed ambitions. My father's handshake, warm and confident that the past was safely buried.

My hands, too, have their kind of confidence, their way of knowing things: where they have been, what they have seen. They have learned their skills not with a sledgehammer, but hovering above a keyboard, deciding what to tell, what to keep back, what to subtract, what to add.

At first, after my strange post-mortal encounter with Harold, my hands didn't want to tell anything. "I," I began, and could go no further. Whatever had happened to that "I" was locked in, too painful to tell.

So the "I" became "Alec" and I wrote about him as though he were not myself but someone else. As though I were relating events that had happened to some stranger. And now, having written them down, having confessed that the stranger is myself, my hands, those nasty power demons, don't want to stop. I could plead — perhaps I have — that it started with my father's hands. *It*. Whatever it was my father did to me. That Harold and I did to each other. What we all did to ourselves. It runs in the family, I could claim, it's only that I use words to do my damage.

But the story of Harold's death begins the day my father was buried. With his funeral and the strange moment in the liquor store parking lot, when Harold and I were smoking cigarettes and in drove the big lime-green swoop-finned Chevrolet with its ruby-studded tail-lights. Because, when the door opened, the woman who emerged was not just some random member-or-not of Harold's fan club who can be passed over in a sentence or two. The door opened and —

"This is Francine," Harold introduced her. "Francine, this is my brother." We didn't even shake hands; she just nodded at me sympathetically. *Francine*, I was thinking, *Francine*, repeating her name over and over to myself. Of course at that moment I didn't know that she would one day reappear as Harold's nurse and then later turn up as his companion at Club Elvis. More. Back at the liquor store parking lot she was just an attractive woman who seemed to know Harold although Harold seemed to be denying it.

When we were finished our cigarettes we went into the liquor store. Francine was already at the cash. She smiled at us. Her eyes were wide-set and a striking golden colour, the kind of gold the Assyrians wore when they came down and struck like wolves on the fold. That was how Francine's eyes struck me. My sheepish heart tore open with a little explosion, I couldn't breathe. The part of me so carefully camouflaged, so supposedly expert at moving only at night and under heavy cover, had suddenly come face to face with someone far wilder, of a whole higher order of danger. I walked past her, telling myself not to stare as I followed Harold to where he was standing in front of a different kind of gold, hundreds of bottles of rye lined up and waiting to be chosen.

We bought two cartons of whisky — a lawyer friend of my father's had given us a wad of fifties so we wouldn't have to embarrass ourselves.

Back at the house, my mother was sitting on a sofa. Her face was puffy and exhausted. Beside her and holding one of her hands piously in his, the rabbi was offering words of consolation. The room was filled with my parents' old friends and a few of our own who had come along for moral support. My father had kept his promise and lived until seventy; his stroke had spared him a second long illness, and there was much muttering that after all his suffering this terrible loss was a mercy, etc.

Perhaps I also felt relief. But mostly pain, distress and anger. Everyone else seemed so calm. I had just won a fellowship that would send me to Europe for more graduate studies. My mother busily spread the word so along with the condolences came a constant stream of congratulations. "Thank you, Mrs. Farmer," I would say. "That's very kind of you, Jack." And even as I was shaking the proffered hand I'd want to grab it, throw the well-meaning fellow-mourner into the wall. Or, pouring drinks, I kept imagining how satisfying it would to hurl the bottle at the window, to break up this false calm with a little blood and shattered glass.

I wondered what my father would think of this tepid requiem. He might have enjoyed it. No doubt if he were here he would be sitting in his favourite armchair, his feet up on the stool, showing off a couple of his golf trophies or asking my mother to get him a glass of milk. For some reason, along with breaking wind and falling in love with the political right, asking my mother to get him a glass of milk had become one of his main hobbies in his last few years. He would walk by the kitchen into the living room, sit down in his chair and then, right away, say to my mother: "Would you mind getting me . . . ." On the day of his own funeral he might have expanded the circle — asked all the apparently obedient wives, and even some husbands and children, to bring him milk. Smiling and contented, he would have been surrounded by a meadow of glasses, taking little sips from each as others reminisced. "And he married a street-stopper," everyone would be sure to say, repeating my father's favourite remark about my mother's fabled and enduring beauty. And my father would nod. "She was. People would actually stop on the street and look at her. Still do."

The crowd began to thin. On the piano was a photographic portrait of my parents taken three years before on their twenty-fifth wedding anniversary. My mother was resplendent in a blue suit, her silver black hair swept back in waves, a dazzling smile directed towards the camera. Beside her, my father, his neck protruding gauntly from a pre-operation white shirt and his favourite brown tweed jacket. He was holding a glass of Scotch and also smiling, but with less dazzle and more puzzlement. "How did I end up with this street-stopper?" he seemed to be asking himself. Had anyone been able to provide an answer —

that he was a man of indescribable qualities; that she liked
the way his slipper heels tap-danced on the kitchen floor;
that he was the rock, she the sea; she the wind, he the flag;
he the thunder, she the rain; he the frog, she the brightly
coloured dragonfly princess, etc. — he would have been
delighted to nod in agreement.

"He had it all figured out," I said to Harold, that very
night after their anniversary. Those were the days, our days.
Harold had been promoted at the agency and was on his
third red car. Saturday afternoons we played in a summer
basketball league and Harold, full of juice, tanned a deep
brown and running five miles every morning, was a *demon*
on the court, a skinny flat-bellied demon who could slap
his fingers against the rim, wire passes half the court's
length, sink his hope-powered jump shots from impossible
corners after which he would stop and laugh, his white
teeth flashing beneath his wide dark moustache. Yes,
Harold was a demon that summer, a demon wolf. After the
game we'd go to the house he'd bought, a small but unde-
niably real house resulting from a big bonus a broker friend
had turned bigger yet, and there'd be a barbecue in the
backyard, Harold with his apron and his steaks and his
cases of beer. Or sometimes the barbecues would happen
at a cottage he'd rented for the summer. I remember one
of those nights sitting on a big rock by the lake with
Harold, the night-time sky punctured by a million dia-
monds, our brains roaring with cocaine. Suddenly, he
leapt off the rock towards the water, his body a perfectly
curved arc. Then he began swimming out, the water slipping quietly past his smoothly moving arms and legs as

though, like my parents, Harold and the water had a secret pact. As Harold swam, others came to stand with me and watch. When he returned and climbed back up the rock we applauded, half ironically — but only half.

Next to my parents' anniversary portrait were pictures of Harold and myself that same summer, the summer of Harold's perfection, and a polished cherrywood bowl half-filled with shelled peanuts, the kind my father always liked. I took a handful; they were stale and too salty. What I really wanted was to get away from this absurd non-wake, but when I looked up to plan my escape I saw more friends of my parents making their way towards me, their eyes ready to brim with tears.

"Fuck," was all I could say to Harold when we finally left my mother's house. It was not yet midnight but my mother was exhausted and some old friends had come from Montreal to spend the week with her.

"Let's get something to eat," Harold suggested.

We drove downtown to a Chinese restaurant we'd started going to in high school when it was the only place we could afford. At the funeral we'd not only drunk our share of rye, but I had taken a couple of walks around the block to smoke reinforced cigarettes provided by a basket-ball friend. Harold too had taken his walks around the block. Now his eyes were puffy and yellow; in the restaurant's harsh light he looked absolutely smashed.

We sat down at an arborite table beside a wall covered with Chinese menus. Harold withdrew his cigarettes and lighter. His fingers were trembling and his eyes were turning moist.

"You okay?"

"Great," Harold said.

A waiter passed with a pot of coffee and I pointed towards our table. The rage I'd been feeling earlier came back, sharp and sour. Why was I so angry? Because the red-faced giant had died, *escaped* before I could level with him? Because I still needed him? But you don't need a reason to be enraged at death. Death is the enemy. Death takes.

"I hated that," I said.

"You should have put in cream," Harold advised. Cream had transformed his own coffee into a muddy brown lake that was slopping over the top of his cup and into his saucer. As he stirred in the sugar, the saucer continued to fill.

"The whatever-it-was after the funeral," I said.

"Did she offer you the suits?" Harold asked.

"The suits?"

"Just after the rabbi left she took me into the bedroom and offered me Dad's suits. Before she calls Goodwill tomorrow."

This reminded me of something I had been meaning to tell Harold: A few weeks ago, when I'd given my parents the news of my fellowship, my mother had offered me money to buy two suits at a downtown tailor. "Students don't wear suits," I'd protested. "You'll need them," she said. "You can't go to Amsterdam dressed like a bum." When she'd said this I could hear my father coughing in the background. No doubt the two of them, after she'd gotten him a glass of milk and herself a sherry, had discussed my coming journey in light of everything they'd read about drug consumption in Europe, and had decided that only official suits could protect me from becoming an addict.

"I told her to give them to you," Harold said, "They wouldn't fit me."

"I've got this," I said. I'd accepted their offer, bought one dark and one light. For the funeral I was wearing the dark. "They paid for it, for school."

"Oh yeah," Harold said. "I thought it was new."

Harold didn't look up. He was slitting the cellophane of a fresh cigarette package with his thumbnail.

"He was pretty fucking proud of you," Harold said.

The waiter was standing above us.

"You want anything?" I asked.

"You order. You're the famous student." This in the contemptuous tone of voice he used when talking about certain "assholes" at the agency.

There was a list of specials that had suddenly become too blurry to read. "Two number threes," I said. "Three is my lucky number."

When the waiter left I took one of Harold's cigarettes. "That was a fucking shitty remark," I said.

"Sorry. What would you like me to say?"

Number three turned out to be one scoop of white rice, one scoop of sweet-and-sour mystery ribs covered in a bright-red gelatinous sauce, and a final scoop of rice, this one mixed with small wrinkled peas and shreds of brown meat.

"He *was* proud of you," Harold said.

"He was proud of you too. He was always telling me how well you'd done without the benefit of a university education. *Without the benefit of a university education,* he would say, waving his milk around. Like the way he used to tell me you had perfect teeth, *without the benefit of braces.* As though I got braces just to stop him from getting a gold locker at the golf club."

"I do have perfect teeth," Harold said complacently. He gave a big smile showing off his absolutely-in-place, cavity-free dental situation.

"There you are. Good-looking. Rich. Plus you could have had Dad's suits. I'm jealous."

"Great," Harold said. He had put his smile away.

Clearly, we'd had two separate fathers, both inhabiting the same body, both dying at once. Now we were going to have to fight over which death was more important. Harold had captured a lump of the rice-pea-meat combination between his chopsticks but, while he was dipping it into the fluorescent sauce, the lump fell apart.

"Shit," Harold said. "Why are we eating this?"

The bill had come with the meal and was waiting in its little plastic tray. Harold put some money in place and stood up.

It was a warm June evening. People were cruising around Chinatown with their windows open, hoping for action or maybe already in the midst of some late-night manoeuvre.

We walked to Harold's current red car, a snappy MG with a great sound system and one missing fender. "You want to come back to my place for a drink?"

"No thanks," I said, but then seeing Harold's suddenly stricken look, changed my mind.

We parked in his driveway. The garage had a basketball backboard and net. I took the ball from the garage and shot a couple of baskets but Harold couldn't be tempted. Inside, he went straight to the kitchen, produced a monster bottle of Scotch and a joint to match. Then we sat in his living room and drank and smoked while Ella Fitzgerald sang to us. Every now and then one of us would mention the name of one of the pets we'd had as children — all brief and tragic encounters — then the other would nod and laugh. When it came to pets we'd had the same father; to him animals were creatures from another planet, to be treated with the kind of distant love and respect you give, say, to mothballs.

After about an hour I realized I was sufficiently drunk or stoned or both that the edge of anger had begun to mellow. Harold was leaning back with his eyes closed, nodding to the music. He had that smile on his face, that smashed shit-eating smile that meant he had drifted out of his body and into the heart of the music, so deep and so pure that the next day he would be able to sit down at the piano and play whatever he had been listening to, his fingers twirling out those grace notes like hyperactive little acrobats. Another joint had appeared on the coffee table between us. I reached for it, but Harold got there first.

I closed my eyes. I was back at the graveside, watching my father's coffin thump into place. *Thump.* Thump thump went my heart like the thumping of his coffin. Like a rowboat thumping across the sand. We'd gone out fishing every morning one summer, my father and I — him rowing, me trolling — the oars thumping against the sides of the boat as he powered us away from our cottage and towards a weedy bay where he would throw down anchor and cast for bass. That weedy bay had a smell I could smell now, a green fishy smell that would get a lot stronger when he caught something. He never held his fish up to the sun the way they do on television. He just brought it to the surface, snapped its neck, then threw it in a cardboard box between us. Now, if it made me feel better, I could think of my father in some huge paradise of a bay, in a boat with a cardboard box filled with black-finned bass.

I stood up and looked at my watch. It was four in the morning. "Time to go," I said.

"Can't," Harold muttered. He opened his eyes wide, the whites large and shiny.

"What's wrong?"

"Feel . . . really . . . bad. . . ."

Harold's lips curved weirdly as he spoke, as though they were about to flutter into uncontrolled babble. He hadn't been floating with the music at all. He was in some kind of bizarre state, hardly able to move. His eyes looked at me questioningly. I bent down, held his wrist to take his pulse.

"Am I alive?"

"Yeah. I'll get you a glass of water."

When I returned, Harold was slumped back in his chair. He drank down half the water, then poured some on his hand and rubbed his face with it. "Feel numb. Do you?"

"Just drunk. I'll make some coffee."

In those days Harold drank instant coffee. The dark brown powder foamed in the boiling water. By the time I'd brought in the steaming mugs Harold had straightened up, was smoking a cigarette.

"We could go to the hospital," Harold said.

"You feeling that bad?"

"Pick up Francine. She gets off soon."

"Francine, the Francine in the parking lot?"

"Francine, the Francine in the parking lot."

I now realized that ever since she'd arrived in her ruby-jewelled Cadillac, Elvis blaring from the speakers, Francine had been with us. Her eyes. The direct way they had looked into mine, the strange angle at which she held herself, the angle that had made me think she was always leaning towards or away from Harold but that was, in fact, just another element of Francine, her constantly changing angle on not just Harold or me but for all I knew the entire world. Or maybe she just liked to have her face in the light.

"Okay," I said and grinned. Harold too. As we stood to go I couldn't help saying, "You know, it's strange you'd say how Dad talked about me as the good student because he once told me you were the one who'd made having children worthwhile." The skin on Harold's face snapped, as though a scorpion had just landed on his cheek.

"Sure."

On the stairwell Harold suddenly stopped and turned me around. At my back was a concrete wall, behind Harold a metal railing. Harold's eyes narrowed and I was filled with a rush of adrenaline. I suddenly felt stoned again, wild and angry, ready to have some absurd battle with Harold in which I would defend the ancient primal rights of the first-born against the treason of the honey-tongued younger brother. Harold's face came closer to mine. It seemed to be throbbing. "Christ," he sobbed. Then he grabbed my shoulders, squeezing hard.

Francine was at the emergency desk, showing her charts to the woman who would be replacing her. There was only one person waiting, a man lying on a stretcher with an intravenous tree attached. He was asleep and breathing loudly, his head to one side, his mouth open; he looked set to spend eternity in this position.

Francine looked up, smiled, then came round the desk to join us. She was wearing a white dress with a white cardigan on top and a small gold chain with a watch around her neck. When she reached us she stood slightly closer to Harold than to me, put her hand on his arm, then leaned slightly, reversing the situation and touching her fingers to my hand. "You survive?"

Harold nodded.

"We have journeyed into the night," I said, and immediately regretted it. Francine smiled, somewhere between irony and forgiveness. In the liquor store I hadn't noticed her hair: it was thick and dark honey-blonde, pulled back from her face, her golden eyes.

"So?" she said to Harold.

"We'll drive you home."

Suddenly the night seemed to have been going on forever. I felt heavy and drunk, but when I asked Harold to drop me at my place he insisted I go with them.

3

Francine's apartment was in a small mid-town building. She had a room-mate who was visiting her parents in Vancouver, she explained as we came into the living room. Harold had brought along his Scotch. While Francine got glasses from the kitchen, I watched Harold try to make himself comfortable in the armchair. He wiggled and squirmed, threw his leg over one chair-arm, then the other, finally leaned back, spread out his arms, began jiggling his knees the way he used to when he was eight years old. With the arrival of drinks Harold toasted first my father, then turned to me and said, "And to Alec, the world's oldest virgin."

Francine laughed. So did I. Although Harold's statement was not precisely true, it might as well have been — in fact, I'd been hoping Amsterdam would provide opportunities to end my long drought. "Too bad your room-mate is away," I said dutifully, and then Harold and Francine laughed again and explained that Laverne was a heavyweight martial arts expert with alternative sexual preferences.

"Just my luck," I said. Harold emptied his glass. I emptied mine. Francine passed us the bottle. Suddenly I wanted to drink until I was drunk enough to put away all the images of my father, his grave, the funeral and the reception afterwards. I drank and I drank and then I started to try explaining all this to Francine. Harold passed out, his face sweetly composed though his head had fallen awkwardly to one side. Francine and I carried him to the bedroom. She had embroidered pillows, and on her neatly arranged dresser were two pink teddy bears with yellow bows around their necks. I helped her take off Harold's shoes and then, while she started to undress him, I returned to the kitchen. I too was drunk. Too drunk. Too drunk to pass out, too drunk to be awake, too drunk to be visiting Francine and too drunk to walk home.

There was a pot of coffee on the counter. I heated it on the stove, ludicrously careful not to make it boil, then washed a mug. The mug was grey with a red heart. I poured the coffee towards the mug; the coffee spilled down the heart, down my shirt front, down the left leg of the dark suit pants my parents had bought me for Amsterdam but had now been worn first at my father's funeral. "Shit," I said, partly because I was annoyed but also because my father always said "shit" when he spilled and I felt I should continue the tradition.

I slurped some coffee and burned my tongue. Then I poured some into the sink and replaced it with a big dollop of Scotch. This was easier on the tongue. I finished one cup of this mixture and started a second.

I was hanging onto the sink, wondering if Harold was naked and dead in the bedroom, wondering what my father would say when he found out I'd let Harold die in a room with two pink teddy bears on the night of his funeral. Everything turned yellow and bilious. My stomach was making itself into a fist. I leaned over the sink, staggered back, fell to my knees. Then began pulling myself up so I could vomit into the sink instead of onto the floor.

I was doubled over the sink when Francine arrived and began dragging me towards the bathroom. "It's where you

want to be," she kept saying. "It's where you want to be."
She was right: I wanted, I wanted to be, I wanted to be in
the bathroom, the door locked, my head in the toilet,
spewing my guts and my grief and the terrible Chinese
food and Harold's Scotch and his joints and the rye I'd
drunk at the funeral along with anything else available; I
wanted, I wanted to spew it up and flush it away so it
would be gone and then I would be an empty bag of skin
which at that moment seemed very attractive.

I knelt in front of the toilet making my strange prayer
but nothing would come. Then I saw the shower. I got my
clothes off, crawled into the shower and pulled myself up
against the wall. When I turned the water on it knocked
me down again. But it felt good, the water, the splashing
onto my face, my hair. Only my feet felt strange. That was
when I realized I was still wearing my socks. I peeled them
off and threw them on the floor where they landed with a
wet smack. I was just propping myself up again when
Francine entered the bathroom. She couldn't have been
too happy to see me like this. She was wearing a big terry-
cloth bathrobe and was holding a toothbrush. I waved to
her, lost my balance, fell face down in the water. This was
good. This was the best. This was like swimming.
Francine's hand was grabbing at me but I pushed her
away. Then she was grabbing again. She had come into
the shower and was trying to pull me up. I still had a bar
of soap in my hand. I reached out to give it to her; I
thought that was what she wanted, but then I saw she had
taken off her bathrobe. "Don't you realize I'm almost
blind?" I said. She was crouched down, looking at me. I

was still offering her the soap, like a peace offering, and since she didn't move to accept it, I rubbed it gently between her breasts. She pushed her hair out of her eyes. I began trying to soap her. She neither helped nor resisted, just crouched there looking at me while I tried to regain my balance. It was crowded. "I can't see and I can't feel," I said. Francine smiled. I had never seen her smile before. At least not with my glasses off, naked and in the shower. "Do you want me to do your back?" I began to turn her around. My hands felt thick on her skin, and I thought how unfortunate it was that at this moment I was so drunk that my hands were too thick to really feel the first naked woman they had touched in several eternities. Then — what luck — the thickness began to drain away. Francine's back pinched to an amazingly small waist, then flared out at her hips. She was turning, or maybe I was turning her, and the skin on my hands had gone from being numb and unfeeling into a pore-to-pore electric dance with Francine when suddenly she slipped and fell on me in a most unusual way. I froze. There was the sound of the shower, the curved wall of water bouncing off Francine's back and onto my face, the spreading heat, an ambiguous hint of movement. I soaped her neck, her shoulder blades, the smooth run of her spine, the cleft between her buttocks. The water was pouring into my eyes, my face, running between us where it could. So much water, so hot, it was hard to know what was the shower and what was us, what was flow and what was movement. I kept soaping. Francine took my hands, made me soap her throat, her chest, her breasts, her belly. Then she took away the soap and pulled my hands down to the place the rest of me was disappearing into. At some point we tipped forward and were on our knees in the shower, doggy-style. Then I was lying on top of Francine, she was facing me, her forehead and cheeks were a bright scarlet and she clamped her legs so tightly around my waist that I exploded into her. A few seconds later I crawled out of the shower and lay gasping on the bath mat. Francine was casually shampooing her hair. Presently she turned off the water, stepped over me and left the bathroom as she'd come in, wearing her bathrobe and carrying her toothbrush.

As I towelled dry, Francine opened the door to hand in a clean pair of jeans and a T-shirt. I put them on, realized they were Harold's, then went out into the kitchen. Francine had made a new pot of coffee and was sitting in her robe, drinking coffee and smoking a cigarette.

"Want breakfast?" Francine asked.

"A piece of toast."

When I was finished my toast and coffee I rolled up my funeral suit and put it in a shopping bag. At her door Francine stood on her toes and gave me a peck on the lips. I'd forgotten to kiss her properly in the shower and now, I knew, I would never have another chance. I wanted to say, "See you in a parking lot," or something equally clever. I wanted Francine to leave her apartment with me, walk out into the morning so we could drive towards the sunrise and begin a wonderful limitless golden life together. "Take care of Harold," I said.

"I will."

The drought was over. I saw myself standing over my father's grave, my hands clasped in front of me, the dark navy cloth of my new suit glinting in the bright June sun, the raw swampy smell of the earth into which my father was descending, the varnished yellow pine of his coffin, my mother's sobbing, the grunts of the gravediggers lowering the coffin into the grave, the silky grain of Francine's skin.

4

By nine o'clock I was at my mother's place. The men from the synagogue had already arrived and, wrapped in tallises, were finishing the mourner's prayer. For a few minutes I stood with them, awkwardly stumbling over the unfamiliar Hebrew words. My mother claimed to have slept but her eyes were darkly shadowed. I stayed with her for a while, then gradually the house began to fill up and I went back home to work. Later that afternoon I dropped by again. Harold had been there earlier, my mother reported. And so it went for the next few days — each time I appeared Harold had just left or was planning to come later. I telephoned his house a couple of times, but he was out.

Two weeks after the night of my father's funeral, I telephoned Francine. When she answered I was unable to speak. She waited patiently, as though accustomed to tongue-tied suitors.

"It's Alec," I finally managed. "Harold's brother."

Francine laughed.

"I wasn't sure if you'd remember my name."

"It's all right," Francine said.

"I just wanted to thank you for —" I wished I hadn't started that particular sentence. How could I have called her without planning what to say? No wonder I had been the world's oldest, etc. "Maybe we could go out for coffee some time."

"I'm working double shifts this week," Francine said, her tone friendly but neutral.

"Okay," I said.

Okay what? I asked myself afterwards. I felt embarrassed and angry. How was I to know if she was Harold's girlfriend or just someone he knew well enough to feel free to go to her place, get drunk and pass out naked in her bed? How could I not have known? I waited two more weeks. Then, late one night, I walked by the hospital, thinking I would "just happen to be in the area" and say hello to her at the desk, at least if there weren't too many people dying in the waiting room. It was about three in the morning; I had spent the whole night trying to find the courage to do this, but as I approached the hospital I spotted Harold's red MG parked across the street. Through the sliding glass doors I could also see Francine. She was wearing a red cardigan — she must have known red was Harold's favourite colour — looking up at Harold and laughing.

All the way home I berated myself. "How could you be such an idiot? A woman, not just any woman, but a nurse who has probably taken some kind of nurse's Hippocratic oath, is trying to save you from drowning and, while rescuing you from your drunken stupor, happens to slip and fall in an unusual way. Does this mean you fall in love with her? Does this mean you spend the rest of your life moping and heartsick? Does this mean you forget you have money to go, absolutely free, to one of the world's most exciting capitals and study with the very man who could explain the historical-cultural-psychoanalytic causes of your inappropriate idiotic response?" Etc. Except that I really *wanted* to see Francine again, take another shower with her, do all those things I'd been thinking about ever since that night.

The next morning I gave my landlord notice and started to pack. It was a month since my father had died. My mother was well taken care of by friends and relatives. The university term would soon be beginning. When I'd received the scholarship I'd had a father, and a brother who was also my best friend. It was time for me to leave before my universe got any smaller. I made my plane reservations and then, two days before I was to go, I telephoned Harold.

"Perfect timing," Harold said.

"For?"

"For you to call. I was just going to call you."

"What were you going to say?"

"I was going to ask if I could use your apartment this afternoon."

"Today?"

"Did you have something special planned?"

"No."

"You see," Harold said, "the problem is that mine's just been painted and the fumes are really bad."

"Sure. Come here then."

"And Francine's room-mate is back, so her place isn't really available."

"No problem here."

"So we'll probably be there about four. David will come about an hour later. We'll bring the sheets and towels."

"Great, are you planning an orgy?"

"An abortion," Harold said. "David's a resident from the hospital but we can't do it there. He tried to get her in for a D and C but that would have taken another month and Francine —"

Harold's voice. Not Harold's usual voice. On the one hand strangely flip and edgy, so much so at first I hadn't believed him. But with every word it got more porous, collapsing into his child's voice, his voice when he fell off his bicycle or got a baseball in the gut.

"You okay for this?" Harold asked.

"Of course."

"You don't have to be there," he said. Then suddenly he was sounding like Harold, my brother Harold, the brother I hadn't heard sound like my brother since the afternoon we were standing in the liquor store parking lot.

"Of course I'll be there. If you want me to."

"I do."

Francine's abortion, later when he was sick, a few times as a child: those were the only times Harold ever asked me for anything. The big emergencies.

They arrived with a sports bag full of bedding. Harold took it straight to the bedroom and began remaking the bed, using a plastic sheet to protect the mattress. Meanwhile, I had put myself in charge of buying liquor, herbal tea, bagels, fruit, paper towels, garbage bags. "Looks like a picnic," Francine said, surveying the layout on the kitchen table. Harold, chain-smoking, came back from turning the bedroom into a chamber of horrors and started a pot of coffee. Francine was the opposite of nervous. This was the first time we'd met since I'd left her kitchen wearing Harold's clothes. Now she smiled at me calmly. Everything about her had slowed. Her hair was luxuriant, her pale cheeks blooming, her golden eyes bright. Francine pregnant was like a fireworks display of beauty. "Don't look so worried," she said. She sat down at the table and started peeling an orange.

Francine's carefully shaped nails, unpolished, digging into the skin, the perfect arch of her fingers as she tugged it free of the flesh, the violent burst of colour as she split the peeled fruit and then her triumphant smile as she offered us the succulent sections, faintly bleeding with juice, that we stepped forward to accept, like disciples at the Last Supper. In the movie, the orange-peeling scene would be beautiful and sad at the same time, a melancholy foretaste of the death to come and, even sitting in the theatre, that foretaste might communicate the tart shock of orange on the tongue, the way it caught in the throat as you realized Francine was certain to die.

"What's wrong?" she now said to me. Harold had stepped out of the room to open the door — I hadn't even heard the knock — but I couldn't answer her because I was thinking of how pale and translucent was the skin beneath her eyes, what a perfect and studied contrast it made with the darkness of her lashes, in fact how perfect, unattainable and untouchable was everything about Francine. Although, of course, in some crucial way she *had* been attained and was now about to be touched in a terrible way. Francine smiled, her head angled towards me, her expression somehow wistful. Why was she having this abortion? I hadn't asked Harold and didn't dare ask her. The obvious reasons? She was too young, too single, etc.? If I were Harold I would have offered her anything to keep the baby.

The doctor, David, looked hatefully unblemished, the kind of person who should be in fashion advertisements. He was wearing a grey suit with pants held up by a snakeskin belt. He shook hands with me when introduced, a firm handshake that reminded me of what his hands would soon be doing. Maybe he was as old as thirty. He had carefully cut blond hair with what was supposed to be an appealing cowlick, a smile full of white teeth, a confident easy way.

"Let's get to it," David said. His voice squeaked. He looked at Harold. "You coming?" Harold nodded. David hefted his doctor's bag, then took a big bowl from the dish drainer. The three of them went into the bedroom and closed the door.

I could hear them talking, the creak of the springs as Francine climbed onto the bed. "Don't look if you're squeamish," David said to one or both of them.

I felt squeamish. I felt I shouldn't hear every noise, every breath. I also shouldn't have been in the shower with Francine. Why was it my fault? It just was. When Margaret and I met and recounted to each other the strange deaths of our fathers along with our various sparse sins, I didn't tell her everything about Francine, just that one night, I'd stumbled on her in the shower. I didn't mention that every detail of Francine's body haunted me for years, that even now I can see the way her skin folds at the edge of her armpits, the tiny pink wedge of tongue between her teeth as she threw her head back, the long scarlet column of her throat streaming with water — detail after unwanted detail that added up to a country too perfect to invent, a country so desirable it moved right into my brain and took up the place labelled "desire" until I got worn out wanting it or met Margaret or both.

I put on some music, unpacked one of my father's glasses and filled it with Scotch. I wondered what my father would think if he saw me here, if he knew the exact situation. I could imagine his face growing suddenly serious, his head nodding up and down as he finally spoke: "I thought something like that would probably happen." Because one of the great things about my father was how he hated the idea that something could surprise him, that there could be an event his mind had not long ago foreseen, analyzed from every angle, tucked away waiting for it to occur so he could sagely nod and murmur that he had seen it coming. I was just picturing the way my father once shook his head while sadly recounting how Elizabeth Taylor had seduced

Richard Burton — "a Shakespearean actor!" — into film when the telephone rang.

"Hi," said my mother. "What are you doing?"

"Nothing. How about yourself?"

"I'm phoning you."

"You're sounding well."

"I'm feeling better. I was going to drop by."

"Better not," I said. "I have to take all my books back to the library today."

"Maybe you and Harold would like to come here for dinner."

"Sure. But I don't know where Harold is. I could call him at work."

"He said he was going to your place."

There was a sudden cry from the bedroom.

"What's that?" my mother asked.

"Something outside."

Harold emerged ashen-faced, carrying the bowl. I pointed urgently at the telephone, then told my mother there was someone at the door and I would call her back this evening. Out came David, supporting Francine, who was wrapped in a blanket. Harold and David led Francine to the bathroom, closed the door behind them. The toilet flushed. Then flushed again. And again. A bright trail of blood glistened on the hardwood floor. "God," Francine said loudly. I rushed to the kitchen, got a cloth and began wiping up the blood. The bedroom door was open. On the bed, on top of the plastic sheet, was a kidney-shaped tray filled with bloody instruments, beside it a large blood-soaked towel. It suddenly occurred to me that it might be two or three months since Francine had gotten pregnant, that I might be entirely innocent of causing this disastrous mess.

Now the bathroom door opened. Harold came out with Francine, still wrapped in a blanket, in his arms. I removed the towel and plastic sheet from the bed. Francine was smiling wanly, and as Harold set her down she reached out to touch me reassuringly.

David reappeared, took the tray and the instruments to the bathroom where he could be heard washing them loudly, the metal clanking nastily. Meanwhile Harold and I sat on the bed, one on either side of Francine, holding her hands. She looked so angelic, so pale, so close to death. She was wearing a flannel nightgown, something from her unimaginable childhood, thick white cotton decorated with red roses and lime-green frogs. "I can see us sitting here," she said. "Like I'm up on the ceiling and I have a halo and I'm ready to float away and there's only you two brothers holding me back." She paused. "The Constantine brothers. The amazing brothers Constantine. You should be a circus act or something. An emergency service for keeping floaters on earth." She looked at us. She smiled. "You're so weird," she said. "The two of you. You have no idea." Harold and I looked at each other and shrugged. We had no idea.

"You're right," I said. "I always think we're the standard and everything else is off. What about you, Harold?" Harold's green eyes were fixed on mine without flinching. Harold definitely had an idea, but what it was, he wasn't saying. Perhaps at that moment he could have become the older brother. Perhaps he did. Then his face relaxed, he gave his eyebrows the old double-twitch he'd long ago perfected, wiggled his moustache.

Francine laughed.

David came into the room. "That was a mess," he squeaked. His smile had bled a little dry, but then he clapped me on the shoulder, winked at Harold, gave Francine a buss on the cheek. "Gotta go."

When David left we were suddenly, the three of us, so alone. We just kept sitting. Francine's words were still sinking in. We might be, as she said, "weird", but her too — the calm Madonna who healed the sick by night, needed it all on the shower floor, then had herself scraped clean. "You're weird," I said to Francine, "and you are so weirdly pure." Francine squeezed my hand, hard. There was an overwhelming feeling of tenderness, we were all close to tears. When Harold was dying it was sometimes like that, the three of us, Francine and I sitting by Harold's bed as he floated through his morphine kaleidoscope; often we would both be touching him at once, Francine and I, massaging, caring, holding. And that same overwhelming tenderness would fill the room, the sacrament of our broken imperfect bodies joining us together, but we never spoke about that other time and if ever Harold and Francine talked about the child that might have been theirs, I never heard about it.

When I couldn't bear it any more I stood up and announced I was going to make Francine some tea. "We'll miss you," Francine said, and everyone laughed. In the kitchen, getting the things ready and waiting for the kettle to boil, I could hear the murmur of their voices. It was so *comforting* to have them in my bedroom, to have their sounds here, part of my life.

My supplies included a package of chocolate marsh-mallow cookies, Harold's old favourite. I arranged them in neat circles on a plate, piled high into a pyramid. I had already sold the table that used to be my kitchen counter and was instead using two heavily taped cardboard cartons which contained the books and papers I'd be needing for my thesis. I set the plate of cookies on top of them while I poured the tea. A few months later in Amsterdam, during one of those evenings when the bottom of the universe seemed to have fallen out, I would try to comfort myself by placing a plate of cookies on these same cartons. It wouldn't work, of course, because Harold and Francine wouldn't be in the next room, waiting for me to arrive with exactly what they needed.

When I brought in the tea and cookies Francine was leaning back against the wall, her eyes closed.

"We were talking about Venice," Harold said. "We met in Venice."

Harold's money had sent him on various exotic trips, including, I now remembered, a three-week excursion to Italy of which I'd seen the slides. Now I remembered one of Harold, standing in some famous church square, wearing sunglasses and grinning at — it must have been Francine. "The picture," I said.

"That was it," Francine took up, her eyes still closed. "He came up to me at a café and asked if he could take a picture of my little boy, Marco."

"I was sincere," Harold protested.

"Of course. But Marco wasn't mine."

"You explained. So I asked if I could take your picture."

"You asked me out to dinner."

"I asked you to go to bed with me."

"I said yes."

"You said it was cheap to go to bed on the first date. That's when I asked you out to dinner."

"I loved that," Francine sighed. "We went to that restaurant on the water. It was candlelight, moonlight, gondoliers poling past. We were sitting by the window. I wanted to be there forever."

"Order good wine, you told me, the kind that lets you drink two bottles."

"I was feeling romantic."

So there they had been. The moon, the candles, two bottles of wine between them, falling into each other's eyes like the sun into the sea.

"I asked you to marry me."

"I told you it was also cheap to get married on the first date," Francine giggled.

"I wanted to be cheap."

"Me too." Francine opened her eyes. They looked at each other in a way I hadn't seen. I picked up the tea things and carried them out. I went to the bathroom, where there was no sign of the blood trail I'd wiped up from the hall. The only abnormal touches were the bowl, perfectly clean, in the bathtub, and beside it a tightly rolled dark-stained towel.

Later, when Margaret was pregnant, she bought a book illustrated with photographs of foetuses at every stage of their development. At two months the entity involved is half an inch long, virtually faceless but its heart developed. Time only makes things more complicated. So I was free to allow my imagination to go back and dwell on those multiple flushings, what or who they had disposed of — along, of course, with the placenta.

Now there is a problem that cannot to be ignored: When the placenta is torn away, the walls of the uterus to which it has been attached do not necessarily heal instantly. A wound has been created, blood vessels open, flesh has been separated from itself. It is against nature, one might say, except that nature includes wounds, blood, death.

I returned to the bedroom, walking quietly this time, not wanting to disturb. Harold was holding Francine's hand again. Her skin was now not merely white, pale or even wan, but absolutely transparent.

Francine opened her eyes. "You want a cookie?" I asked.

"You look like Robin Hood," Francine said.

She had no way of knowing, but I have always had an obsession with Robin Hood, the way he had almost bled to death before anyone noticed — by which time it was too late. Now I could smell blood. I lifted up the cover. The bed was soaked.

This was the beginning of my first ambulance moment. Eventually I would realize the incredible significance of this moment, the fact it is one we must all experience. I would even write a book in which the hero is constantly listening for sirens. The hero was Harold, of course — Harold disguised as me in order to amuse him. Harold made the phone call. I gave Francine a glass of water. Before she could finish it the ambulance arrived, siren blaring. By the time I got downstairs, a crowd had already gathered around the door. Two minutes later their curiosity was satisfied: Francine, lashed to a stretcher, was carried out of the building. As the attendants lifted her up into the ambulance Harold turned to me. The careful planning, the cultivated optimism, Dr. David's assurance had all dissolved. With them, Harold's masks. The scorpion had bitten; Harold looked raw and afraid. He followed Francine into the back of the ambulance, then turned to me one last time. "Excuse me," he said gently, "while I shut the door in your face."

As the ambulance accelerated away from my apartment and towards the hospital, the siren went on again. Like everyone else I stood dumbly, watching it disappear into the traffic. Then I turned and went in my own door, locking it behind me.

Upstairs I washed up the dishes, put the bloody laundry into garbage bags, recommenced packing. It was seven in the evening. In exactly twenty-four hours I would be on an airplane, heading for Europe. I spread my suitcases out on the mattress that the plastic had so thoughtfully spared. The telephone rang. My mother was wondering why she hadn't heard from me about supper. I explained that Harold was busy but I would be over shortly. I went into the bathroom to wash my face. The night after my father's funeral, when I was so drunk, I wanted to bring up but couldn't. Now it was easy. In fact compulsory.

"You're looking terrible," my mother said as I came in. "You're going to too many parties."

5

So there I was. At my mother's for dinner while Harold was at the hospital watching Francine live or die. I had not arrived empty-handed. I had brought her a copy of *White Men Dying*, by my mentor-to-be, Dr. Herbert Franz Strauss Meyser, the man after whom I would one day name Harold's hat.

Herbert Franz Strauss Meyser! What a name! What a monicker! No wonder he made sure to put "Doctor" at the front — something to warn or distract or push aside the cheering throngs.

I was put on the trail of the amazing Dr. Meyser and his first book by a downtown Toronto bookstore clerk, a friend of a friend. I was living in my apartment and dreaming elaborate dreams. Harold had his red car. I had started graduate school and was in search of a cause. The clerk's fingernails were chewed to the quick. He looked not at me but at the ceiling as he talked, then climbed a stepladder to pluck it down from a top shelf. As I received this fateful gift I, too, looked at the ceiling. "The European male is a black-cloaked dinosaur shuffling towards extinction," I read when I got home. I was twenty-three years old. I had no beard, only sideburns. The idea that the world's ruling class was a self-deluding imperialist mutation about to crash into oblivion was not unwelcome. I didn't want to rule the world. I didn't even want to rule the people I knew. I just wanted to go to bed with some of them, stay up all night getting sweaty — screwing, talking, being excited — then run outside when the sun came up to watch it make the fabulous pale ghosts of houses real again, to see the street fill with people and cars, and restaurants with the sharp sizzle of breakfast, strong coffee to start everything all over.

Without his knowledge or consent, Dr. Herbert Franz Strauss Meyser became the object of a miniature cult among three or four of my fellow students at the University of Toronto. When by fluke I won the fellowship to travel and study abroad, he seemed a natural destination.

In the weeks since my father had died, my mother's steps had gotten shorter and heavier. Although she had plans. As soon as things were "sorted out", she said, she was going to work part-time escorting children's school tours at the museum. I remembered going to the museum with my own school. On these annual excursions we were always met by one or another elegant retired lady who would show us the dinosaurs and the totem poles. These ladies — they were so clearly "ladies" — seemed themselves to be both fossils and totems, encased in lacquered hair, carefully pressed suits, painted faces and nails, precise hard-edged voices. My mother, I thought, was still a decade or so too young to qualify. But I didn't object. Instead I told her about the thesis I was planning to write on the collapse of male supremacy, civilization, the rise of rock and roll, my great fortune in being permitted to learn at the feet of the brilliant Dr. Meyser; then my mother told me about the sleeping pills she was refusing to take, the way she kept waking up at six in the morning, coming out into the living room and thinking she had nothing to do.

"Of course I have a lot to do," she laughed. "I've sent away his clothes, now I'm packing up his books and papers. I'm going to put them in boxes so you can have them when you come back. You'd like that, wouldn't you?"

"Of course," I said. I still have those books, carefully stored in the basement, waiting for some future archaeologist. The golf trophies are in my study. They're bright and shiny and the children used to play with them.

We sat down at the table. My mother had heated one of the frozen casseroles people brought around after the funeral. I suggested we have a glass of wine.

"I don't think I've ever had dinner with you before," my mother said. "Not just you." She smiled. "What have you got to tell me?"

"I just told you my whole thesis."

"Tell me about yourself. For example, do you have a girlfriend?"

"No one," I said.

"You never go out on dates?" She had finished her first glass of wine and was having a second. My mother is one of those people for whom the second glass is the point of no return.

"Mom," I protested.

"Tell me."

"I go out on dates."

"What do you do?"

A week before my father died, I'd been "on a date" with a woman I'd met at the library, but so much had happened since, I'd forgotten about her. "It wasn't exactly a date. Not official. But a student I know asked me to read an essay she'd written, then we went for coffee."

"That's all?"

"It wasn't just a regular coffee, it was a cappuccino." In fact, after the cappuccino we'd gone back to her place and smoked dope. Then she put on a jazz record and explained to me that her boyfriend had gone to live in England for a few months. "That's too bad," I'd said. "Maybe I'm glad," she'd replied. "Oh," I'd said. "I just thought I should tell you," she'd said. "Maybe you want to think about it before we see each other again."

"Then what?"

"She proposed to me," I summarized.

My mother laughed. "You see? You're better looking than you think. If you just did something about those glasses. Why don't you try contacts? And those clothes, God, let Harold take you shopping; Harold knows how to get girls. Is she Jewish?"

My heart was feeling, as they say, heavy. Filled with dread and anxiety, huge and distended, so literally heavy that it wanted to fall down through my chest into my stomach. I got out a rolaid and managed to eat it while my mother had her back turned to fill the kettle. But she caught me refilling my wine glass.

"It's a good thing you're not driving," she said.

"It's a good thing I don't have a car. I'd just have to sell it."

"You're going to need a car when you get married. You can't spend the rest of your life living in the same apartment."

"I'm leaving for Europe tomorrow."

"You know what I mean. You remember how Dad always said you would have to learn to look out for yourself."

"I do look out for myself."

"People take advantage of you."

"Who takes advantage of me?"

"Billy Wheaton used to. You let him copy your homework but you were the one who got caught."

I wondered if I was having a heart attack. Or just bleeding to death inside. Then suddenly Harold walked in. He had showered and changed, his smooth face glowed with happiness and relief.

"Hey, you ate without me! And look at this!" He picked up the half bottle of wine and went through his comical eyebrow-raising routine before getting himself a glass. "So?"

"Alec was telling me about his thesis. It was very interesting. And his new girlfriend."

"New girlfriend? Is she Jewish?"

When he drove me home, Harold told me that Francine was resting comfortably, that she had lost blood but not needed a transfusion.

"So that's it?"

"That's it," Harold said.

We were parked outside my apartment. I couldn't face going back upstairs alone, but nor did I want to invite Harold. I felt as though I'd been used as some sort of rag, to wipe and absorb the dirt of the thing, and was now being thrown away.

"What happens next?"

Harold shrugged. He was drumming his fingers on the wheel, then stopped himself by lighting a new cigarette. He was high on the excitement and the danger, ready for action. "What happens?"

"With you and Francine."

"We'll have to see about that."

The next morning I went to visit Francine. She was sharing a room with a huge and obviously very uncomfortable woman who must have had some terrible kind of surgery. While I was there doctors came and went, closing her curtain and doing things that made her groan. When the curtains would open she would be slumped on her aside, apparently asleep.

Francine looked good. Slow and pale, but with a touch of colour in her cheeks. I pulled a chair close to her bed, and in the intermissions between the groans from next door Francine told me they had performed a D and C, and that once recovered from the anesthetic she could go home.

"That's great," I said.

"You were great," Francine said.

"You were," I said. Maybe I wanted her to cry. Her eyes were misty but calm. She was calm. Untouched after all.

She wasn't going to end up with Harold, I realized. She and Harold were in some other sphere, a sphere immune to the holding power of love, a sphere in which passion was like the two bottles of wine you could drink because you only drank good wine, wine that didn't give you a hangover.

"Goodbye," I said. I was back in the movie where the beautiful heroine peels an orange; this was my cue, time for the foolish drunk in the shower to get out of the way so the main action could begin.

"I'll be seeing you," Francine said. "Write to me." Her golden hair an aura on the pillow.

I backed out of the room, feeling very bad.

When Harold arrived to drive me to the airport he was in the best of moods. It was contagious. We were in his red car, piled high with my luggage, we were zooming out of town, away from Francine, away from everything that needed to be left behind. Harold didn't even mention Francine — he talked about a new twelve-string guitar he'd just bought with a bass register that made your skeleton tremble, a new camera that was on the floor in front of me and that he was going to use to take my picture as I left Toronto in order to study the collapse of civilization.

We got to the airport early enough to go the bar. We had a couple of drinks. Harold had me with him now on the optimist's highway, the bright shining highway to the better brighter future. We found a volunteer to photograph us together. We were wearing sideburns and sunglasses and had cigarettes sticking out the corners of our

mouths as part of an elaborate joke in search of a punchline. Harold wore his big wide smile and I was trying to
raise a single eyebrow to indicate the rich crazy unknow-
able irony of it all.

IT is December. Harold squints into the snow. The grey sky. Listens to the sound of tires splashing through the slushy streets. The last traces of fall have disappeared beneath the rising tide of Christmas. A Santa Claus is working his way towards him, weaving through the stacked crates of Chinese vegetables, staggering with each step as though about to collapse. His red uniform is crumpled and stained, his beard lopsided. From his neck hangs a tin can inviting donations. For those who don't like cans, Santa Claus is holding out his hands. "Alms for Christmas, I have no home. Alms for Christmas, I have no home. Alms for Christmas, I have no . . ."

He stops in front of Harold. "Please. I'm going to die of the cold." Then his eyes, an impossibly washed-out blue centred by hard black pupils look straight into Harold's face. Despite the snow, Harold is sweating. He digs into his pocket for change while the Santa Claus tries to steady himself. Then the Santa lurches forward, grabs Harold's money and moves on.

The air smells of fish and crushed oranges. Overflowing from the sidewalk are vans with their rear doors angled open, dollies stacked with cartons, clerks and passers-by jostling for space. A wet snow is slowly falling, everyone is wearing down vests, ski parkas, fur hats.

In their midst Harold is tall and slender, coatless in his dark suit, white shirt open at the collar. His exposed triangle of neck is pink and glistens with sweat, his face drawn and tense. For a moment the tips of his fingers meet and flex; then he reaches into his suit jacket and his hands busy themselves with a cigarette.

Sick, he lost the desire to smoke. Also the small anxious tremor that must have invaded him before he was born, a half-broken wild horse he spent his whole life riding. Now he could smoke or not. Like anything else. Nothing like dying to put iron in a man's soul. Nothing like six months lying blind in your own coffin to make you appreciate the tiniest of pleasures.

Smoke claws at his lungs, but his blood is calm. These days it can be hard to know in what order to take things. Or the whole situation. He wonders if he will talk to Alec about that, about the whole situation. Alec always favoured big ideas, the big picture. Harold gets a picture of Alec: short, compact, bristly black hair with a lawn-mower cut, glasses so thick and heavy they are always sliding down his nose, dark eyes he used to practise holding open so he could stare unblinking at people while telling them lies. "Natasha, this snow *will* melt." Or: "I *do* care what happens to you." Chipped tooth, chippy personality. Always ready to take offence. Terrible dresser. Always used to be broke, holier-than-thou. Did too many drugs.

Harold is standing in the middle of the sidewalk, thinking about his brother, the reformed family man, the big-
time professor and journalist, almost. He knows what he
wants to say to Alec, Alec the softie, Alec who only lies
because the truth is too harsh to bear. He knows what he
wants to say but the words keep slipping away.

With his mother, words had been no problem. When
the cancer got bad she started coming to see him every-
day. He would hear her slow resigned step on the stair, her
short, half-stifled gasps of shock and despair, and then with
the one official sigh she was permitted she would lower
herself beside the coffin that was pretending to be the hospital bed in which they could take care of him more
easily, if care was what they were taking. Sometimes,
watching the comedy his mother forced herself to play, he
had to struggle to keep himself from smiling at her
predicament — those were the rare days, the days he felt
well enough that his mother would have been glad to
know he was laughing at her efforts to contain herself,
laughing at anything — but mostly he felt black and heavy
inside, choked-up with his own stifled gasps, with his infi-
nite regret for the pain he was causing her.

"It's me," she would say, because she had to say something and she didn't want, for example, to ask him how he
was — what would that leave him? — though eventually
she would, when the context had surrounded, cushioned
and limited the question to something he could answer
with "fine", or "not bad", or "better" or even a negative
nod, a nod to show it was a bad moment, but nothing too

serious aside from the fact that he was blind and dying in agony, just a passing catastrophic plunge after which the steady decline would continue.

"Well," his mother would then say, "I heard something interesting on the radio today." Or: "How about those Expos? Down two in the ninth and they come back. Do you want me to read you the sports?" Or: "You'll never guess who I ran into in the supermarket today. She wants you to know —"

> Tell her you saw me
> Don't tell her where
> Tell her I miss her
> Tell her I care
>
> Tell her to trust
> Our secrets won't rust
> Next to my heart
> In a locket of hair

That had been the rage for a while, those weeks in his coffin that was pretending to be a hospital bed: putting together little rhymes, bitter greeting card verses to send to the living. Though he didn't, of course, send them. Or even hum them.

> Had a dog
> Who wore a wig
> Made him look
> Like a hunchbacked pig

Lost his tail in the middle of his bowl
Won it back on a lucky roll

The clouds had thinned to a grey-blue tinted yellow by
the emerging sun, but the snow was still falling, falling
harder, gusts of large wet flakes that melted as they landed
on his face and shoulders.

Suddenly Harold remembered a Saturday afternoon
he and Alec were playing shinny on a neighbourhood
rink. Alec with his sharp and useful elbows had sent a
bigger kid falling against the boards. The victim, over six
feet tall and towering above Alec, had looked with amaze-
ment at the small fool who had tried to humiliate him. He
got to his feet, waited until Alec came close, swung his
stick like a baseball bat into Alec's mouth. Alec's face
covered in blood. Alec, unbelieving, wiping it off with his
hand, putting snow on the wound to stop the bleeding.
The snow turning from white to red, then dripping to the
ice. Large scarlet splashes tracing Alec's path from centre
ice to the door at the side of the rink.

That had been a day. The day Alec had walked into
Club Elvis. As soon as he was in the door Harold knew he
was there. Felt the wild quiver of Alec's curiosity. Got in
line with the others while the Nymphets crooned. That day
there was a sweetness in their voices — if he ever got to
heaven would there be sweetness like that? Alec's eyes had
fastened on him; they were literally glowing in the dark,
trying to stare right through him. Alec moving closer. So
wounded. He hadn't wanted to wound Alec. He hadn't
wanted to wound anyone. Hadn't wanted to get sick.

The look on Alec's face as he stared. Like the first time he had seen Alec after telling him about the cancer. The way he'd stared at him, trying not to.

"How are you?" Harold had asked. And at that moment he'd been worried not about himself but about Alec, the stricken expression on his face, his eyes that didn't know how to take in what they were seeing.

"How are *you*?"

"Not bad."

> Tell her I wore that bird till it stuck
> Tell her I died with my bird on
> Tell her the feather ate the weather
> Tell her my coffin is too small
> Tell her dying is like a mirror only
>   the dying can look into

MERRY CHRISTMAS banners hung above the streets. Store windows were adorned with Santa Claus figures, sprayed snow, ivy-bordered advertisements. Even the second-hand bookstore had a rectangle of blinking lights surrounding a CHRISTMAS SALE sign. Inside the bookstore Harold moved automatically to the C's. There was Alec, both his novels. Harold pulled one out, opened it. The first blank page was missing. That meant, Alec had explained to him once, that the book had been a review copy and that the reviewer had torn out the page stamped NOT FOR RESALE before selling it.

The book was so new that the spine cracked. The critic hadn't even read it, Harold realized, and his face flushed with anger on his brother's behalf. Then, feeling as though he had intruded on something, Harold put the book back and glanced over at the counter. A black-haired woman was sitting on a stool, apparently engrossed in a crossword puzzle. If she had any negative thoughts about a dead person coming into her store and looking for his brother's books, she was keeping them to herself.

Harold moved to a different aisle, found a well-thumbed copy of the 1989 *Baseball Almanac*. He turned to the section on the Expos. Even more than going to the games, he had liked listening to them on the radio. At night in a car, driving towards the cottage, sky turning liquid blue. In the afternoon at the office. Lying in bed in the dark, like a kid.

The sounds of coaches and players calling from the dug-out, the beautifully blank pause between the pitch and the moment when the bat cracked into the ball, the announcer's hoarse excitement, the rising cries of the fans as that unseen ball floated towards its unknown destination.

Out on the street again the sun glared off the snow. Harold put on his sunglasses, the old-fashioned kind with mirrored lenses. A cold wind had started up and a skin of ice had started to form on the sidewalks. Harold jammed his hands into his pockets. He was standing in front of a store with women's sweaters. There was a mannequin draped in a rich-looking, deep red cardigan. On Francine it would look even better. Francine had given him her credit card, but he couldn't buy her a Christmas present with her own money. Maybe he would see Alec soon. Alec would give him money. Or he could get a Santa Claus outfit and a can for begging on the street. That would be something. Maybe he would run into some of his old clients. The big tippers. "Reminds me of Harold," they'd say to themselves, pressing wads of bills into his palm. Or they wouldn't.

When he got to the club, Francine was waiting for him, reading a newspaper. As he sat down she reached out for his sunglasses, put them on. Then Francine bounced her eyebrows up and down and this made the mirrors bounce with them. In their reflections Harold saw his own face, wan and angular. "Unfair," he said. "They look better on me."

"No they don't. They make you look cheap. They make you look like the kind of person who goes to bed on the first date."

"Excuse me," Harold said, "while I shut the door in your face," and their hands came together as they laughed.

The stage was dark now, empty except for a dead microphone and a stool positioned in the centre. It was so strange the way it had happened. He had just come to. Opened his eyes and found himself leaning against a lamppost on Queen Street. It was evening. Cars were going by, their headlights much brighter than he remembered. It was fall, one of those crisp nights that used to be laced with the smoke of burning leaves. He'd been leaning against the lamppost getting used to the brightness of the lights and he thought, might as well stand up straight. Then he had started walking, through this purgatory or heaven or hell or whatever it was. The bars and restaurants seemed familiar.

He was wearing a black suit, one of his favourites from before he got sick. Maybe they'd buried him in it. He reached into his pockets for cigarettes. There was a fresh package. He opened it up. Snapped his lighter. A streetcar rattled by. Faces peered out at him. Were they on their way to St. Peter? Who knew? He waved and kept on strolling. That was when he saw it, the sign. CLUB ELVIS. Nancy or someone had told him about this place, he now remembered, or thought he did. Suddenly thirsty he patted his back pocket to make sure he had his wallet. That same empty stool had been in place, a spotlight shining on its varnished seat. He had the crazy idea that seat was waiting for him. He walked towards it. Sat down and looked around the club. No boos, no applause. No anything. Then the lights dimmed and he was able to see.

"Over here."

He'd peered into the shadows, towards the voice. Francine, sitting at a side table. He'd gone to join her.

"Is this really happening?"

"I think so," Francine had said. And then she had smiled and it was as though she had thrown his power switch. ON.

Now he was seeing his pale reflection in the mirrored sunglasses. He had a cigarette in his mouth but it wasn't lit.

Francine looked over to a waiter, pointed to Harold's cigarette. The waiter held up a lighter. Harold raised his arm. His wrist was so skinny it hardly seemed capable of supporting anything, let alone a fairly large human hand.

"Go ahead," Harold said.

The lighter, a blue plastic tube, tumbled through the air. Harold closed his fingers around it as it arrived, then winked at the waiter. "Well thrown," he pronounced gravely, as though he had toured every bar and tavern on the continent, testing the throwing skills of pretenders to the throne this man so clearly occupied.

"We could play the game," Francine said.

"Venice."

"Where in Venice?"

"We're sitting on the edge of the Grand Canal."

"And then?"

"You ask me to take you out to dinner."

"What kind of dinner?"

"A good dinner. Seafood and grilled artichokes and wine that makes you want to order a second bottle because your mouth tastes like flowers and you know you won't get a hangover."

"Done."

Outside the sun had disappeared. The clouds hung black and low, full of the snow that was falling again. Harold was standing in front of another store window, the soles of his feet burning in the slush that had soaked through his shoes. Beneath an arc of yellow paste-on stars, dozens of perfect snowflakes were artistically suspended above a wicker cradle in which a doll of the baby Jesus lay beneath a colourful quilt. Mary, on her knees, looked at him adoringly while Joseph sat in a rocking chair, appropriately dubious.

"You see those eyes?" rasped a voice.

Harold turned. The question came from a heavy-set man wearing a stained canvas parka. His face was shaven painfully close, his nose a slowly exploding warning against drinking cheap whisky.

"Stupid eyes. Not a real blue. Fucking shit."

"I guess so," Harold said. He took out his cigarettes. Offered them. The man helped himself, bent to Harold for a light.

"A baby's eyes, they have a special blue. Like the sky. Summer sky, you know what I mean?" He paused and looked at Harold. His eyes might once have been baby blue, but now they were a bloodshot brown tinged with yellow. He leaned close to Harold, let his mouth drop open. His breath washed over Harold's face. "I had a baby once. Eyes like the sky in July." Suddenly he turned and pointed to a window above the store. "That's where we lived. Right there. Inside. Every day I walk past that fucking window."

> Knew a man who lived downtown
> Had a baby wore a crown
> One long night that baby died
> Now he drinks the tears he cried

"You know what happened to that baby?"

"I think so," Harold said.

"Look at you," the man now said.

"Me?"

"You look dead. Man, you look dead. You are a real fucking mess. You need some of that." He pointed to the baby. "Jesus Christ, man. Jesus in your soul. Jesus *is* in your soul. Did you fucking know that?"

"No," Harold said.

"Don't fuck with me. *No*. You some kind of private school asshole? You look like a bum. Only difference is I got Jesus in my soul and I know it. You got Him but you don't."

A slim white arm came into view in the window, gold bracelet on the wrist, a small carefully kept hand. It began placing ceramic animals and magi around the cradle.

"Jesus died for our sins," the man said.

"That's great."

"What do you mean, *that's great*. It *is* great. It's fucking wonderful. He died for our sins and then He rose from the fucking dead. Is that fucking incredible or what?" The man had grabbed Harold's coat, was holding Harold close.

"You're spitting," Harold said. "It isn't polite to spit."

"ANSWER ME OR I'LL KILL YOU! DO YOU WANT ME TO KILL YOU, YOU ASSHOLE?"

"No," Harold said. He pried the man's fingers away from his jacket. His eyes strayed to the window where the man said he had lived with his baby. The window was covered with gauzy white curtains. He could see the woman behind those curtains, an exhausted woman slumped in an over-stuffed armchair watching afternoon soaps on one of those old-fashioned television sets enclosed in dark scarred wood and crowned with rabbit ears. The infant in her arms. Lips, curved around her nipple, rimmed with tiny white milk bubbles.

Suddenly the man drew back his fist and swung at Harold's face. Harold stepped back. The man stumbled and fell to his knees in the slush.

Harold had a sudden image of Alec at the hockey rink, his hand on his face, blood running between his fingers. The sound of a satisfied curse in the icy air as the boy who'd hit him wheeled away, banged his stick in triumph on the ice as though he'd just scored.

When Harold got back to Francine's, he took off his jacket. Then he went to the bathroom to get a drink of water. His face in the mirror was dead white, each beard hair a black accusing needle.

Now he was sweating again. He started a bath, poured in bubble gel so he wouldn't have to see himself in the water. But as he got undressed he couldn't help looking down at his legs. The sickness had stripped away most of his flesh and his legs were so thin that each movement made his muscles pop about unnaturally, as though he was one of those marathon runners he had once used for a soft drink commercial.

A few minutes later he was in the bath, body soft and supple, humming with satisfaction. Soaping himself, he arched his spine. When he was sick, the salt from his sweat used to dig into his useless eyes. He would imagine his sweat building up, overflowing his face, filling the room, sending him floating out the window, away from the others who kept standing over him, waiting for him to die; away from the drugs that made his muscles spasm and cramp; away from the morphine pump; the volcanic bedsore perched on his left hip like a permanent vulture eating into the bone; the garbage bags of shit; the bottles and bottles and bottles of pills; the shark cartilage powder recommended by homeopathic therapists who could also cure cancer by injecting secret formulas into your groin; the garlic-fried parsnip; the pain wired into his bones.

When he stepped out of the bath, water streamed from his body as though he were a Greek statue poised in a fountain.

"Have I risen from the dead or what?" Harold said, and his voice echoed in the bathroom. Somehow he had come out of the bath and returned not to purgatory but to what was natural, the nature zone, the erogenous zone, the youth zone, the zone he had somehow fallen out of because he got too sick or too tired or too dead or too busy or just unlucky.

Into his mind came a picture of himself standing on his hands. Slowly Harold bent down, lowered his fingertips to the floor, his body flexed and vibrating. Slowly, in a beautifully controlled slow trickle, his weight flowed up from his feet, through his legs and groin, around his belly and down through his spine, his shoulders, then down his arms and into his hands that were pressed against the cool tiles of the bathroom floor. At the precise moment that all his weight came into his hands, his feet left the ground and began to float upward.

Harold counted to a hundred. Still on his hands, he walked across the tiles and started into the bedroom where the carpet was a dense faded green he hadn't really noticed. From where he stood he had an excellent view of the underside of the bathroom sink. Blue rubber gloves hung from the plumbing. He turned around. His spine felt firm and balanced, as though prepared to stay this way forever. Francine had come in while he was in the bath. She was sitting on the bed, reading the paper.

"Look at me."

"Feeling better?" Francine asked without looking.

"Feeling great," Harold said. "*Look* at me." He watched Francine's eyes lift from the paper and focus on where his head should be, before travelling down to take in the whole picture.

"That's great," she said in a voice that was totally indifferent.

Harold looked at the carpet. The fibres had melted together. He was miraculously poised on the surface of a warm green ocean. Then the surface gave way and closed over him, his body smooth white marble gliding through the dark underwater mountains.

1

HAROLD in his dark Italian suits. The way his fingers were always moving. The sudden open flash of his palms. The burst of applause after yet another of his amazing tricks — in fact, his most amazing trick of all — his disappearing trick. How did he do it? Well, Ladies and Gentlemen, you had to be there. You had to buy a ticket. You had to witness it in slow motion, the astonishing moment when the master magician actually passes through the most invisible of doors. In being the first to die Harold was defining death for those of us who would follow him — and we all will. *This is dying*, Harold was saying, but though he had been condemned to death for no particular reason, Harold was engaged in an intense struggle to yield his body only as fast as he could secure his soul — the only armour he would have to protect him in the next phase of his journey, his fall into nothingness.

Meanwhile my heart, the heart that is to be laid bare. Rusted drums begin their roll, the faded velvet curtain twitches. My heart blushes. If only there were a lacy white

petticoat it could pull over its red pulsing self. If only it
could have a few drinks and retreat. If only —

My heart, the heart that is to be laid bare, floats
through time and space, dreading the fateful encounter.
Trailing bits of veins and arteries, losing a little more
blood than it should, wheezing on the hills; my heart is
broken but not smashed, bereft but not vacant, bruised but
not numb. The day Harold told me he had cancer, I
thought I would die. In that room of the Hotel Ambassade. Leaning over the telephone. Hearing those impossible words. I thought I would die while I was hearing
them and after I heard them I thought I would die before I
could leave the room. SHOCK SLAYS MAN HEARING OF
BROTHER'S ILLNESS. Or drinking the beer I finally
ordered from room service. DEAD WRITER FOUND
CLUTCHING BOTTLE IN AMSTERDAM HOTEL ROOM. Even
months later, playing basketball in the gym where we used
to go together, I would sometimes feel my bruised heart
gripping itself like a fist, desperately hanging on; and I
would think, *My heart is going to break*. But I didn't die,
Harold did. I was left behind to mourn, to puzzle it out, to
rediscover him at Club Elvis and then lose him again.

It was, to be exact, the 21st of November when I met Harold,
very definitely deceased though obviously not dead in the
normal way, at Club Elvis. On the 22nd I returned, met
him again, accompanied him and Francine to the beach.
On the morning of the 23rd they disappeared. After that I
returned to Club Elvis several times — at least to where it

once had been. The second-hand bookstore was still in place, but the CLUB ELVIS sign was gone. The narrow pathway led to a door which opened unlocked to a dilapidated house carved into apartments. There was a row of mailboxes in the hall — most of them stuffed with junkmail and telephone bills. I stood in that hall, inspecting the names on the boxes for some kind of clue. Upstairs a dog began to bark. I crossed the street, stood watch. Eventually an old woman emerged, dragging a two-wheeled shopping cart. I followed her for a while — she was collecting empty bottles and cans.

One afternoon I went back to the beach. The sand was packed, half-frozen, an icy wind blew in off the water, gulls wheeled and cried in the cold. On this chilly day, there was only one jogger, a determined and enterprising young mother pushing a stroller as she trotted along, singing to her squalling child. Absolute absence of Harold.

Now it is December 18th — 10:22 p.m. to be exact — twenty-five shopping days since I went to fetch coffee for Harold and Francine and less than seven shopping days until Christmas. I am sitting in my basement office, typing these words into my computer.

What next? Where can I possibly go from here? Scattered on my desk, lying on top of worthier projects — essays to be marked, bills to be paid, notes for my book on the decline of everything, and the beginnings of a review I am to write of Dr. Meyser's latest and greatest — are yellow sheets of paper labelled Option 1, Option 2, Option N, Option Z, Option Etc.

Option 1: Do myself a favour, erase what I've written on this machine, go see a qualified psychiatrist or necromancer.

Option 2: Be a man, assume my responsibility as a writer, make this an uplifting story suitable for posterity: i.e., change it into the tale of two Jewish brothers whose hobby is helping old ladies across the street and doing other good deeds.

Option N: Employ the famous "digression technique". This is particularly useful at parties. When someone you don't like starts to tell a story, you join the crowd, apparently listening closely and chuckling in appreciation of the rich comedy to come. Then, just as the hated narrator approaches the crucial moment, you interrupt with a tiny little remark that starts a few people giggling. Annoyed, the storyteller glares at you, then recommences. You wait a couple of sentences, then strike again. If necessary repeat several times until the listeners are in hysterics and your enemy has gone from being the centre of attention to the thick-headed straight man for your comical asides. By this time he will have forgotten his own story; instead he will be wondering how he could have been stupid enough to start a story with you in the room. This is a trick I have often performed — invariably on myself, while I am writing. Every sentence is mined with a subtext that means its opposite, every paragraph strays from its alleged topic. "Just write down what you have to say and get it over with," a sympathetic editor once advised me. Good idea. If only I knew what I was supposed to be saying. Then I could arrange it in neat little paragraphs, preferably set down in alphabetical or at least logical order. But if I have something to say it is too provisional to be named. Or it's that life is too confusing to pin down, or it's that Harold has hidden the punchlines in his black attaché case. Successful writers have steely gazes and refuse to flinch at ambiguity. Which reminds me — but that would be a digression from the digression and all this wavering of purpose is why I am typing this in a basement "office" that is also the laundry room, on a desk that is also an old door, instead of on a hunk of teak screwed into the jungle-wood floor of a luxury yacht. On the other hand Shakespeare did get away with Rosencrantz and Guildenstern. Forget Harold. Maybe now is the time to tell about my life in Amsterdam, Doctor Meyser's theory that Faust died with the invention of television, and so on.

Option z: Remember Harold. Forget this. Shut off the computer and make yet another trip down to Queen Street to see if Harold has reappeared.

Option Etc.: Admit that I have no idea what to do, that in fact I have no intention of doing anything, admit that I believe there has been a terrible mistake: when I answered the hotel telephone cosmic circuits crossed and I was somehow expelled from reality.

In the real and normal world, the one from which I have been mistakenly exiled, Harold is alive and well. It is eternal summer, I am walking down the street with Simon and Emily, hand in hand in hand. Margaret, just ahead of us, is turning to say something and as she speaks I am noting for the ten-millionth time with what soft Renaissance splendour her lips frame themselves around each

word, how smoothly her glowing skin blends into the red
bricks of the houses on our street, how harmonious are the
late-afternoon clouds infused by the same light that illumi-
nates her eyes. From an invisible orchestra of ten-thousand
strings, romantic music begins to swell. I step close to
Margaret as she speaks, slide one of my hands into her
back pocket, and as she returns the pressure the children
wedge themselves between us. In that perfect world, that
real world I've somehow left, the children will eat dinner,
play educational games and read worthwhile books, while
Margaret and I drink a bottle of wine. Harold will call to
invite us over for a barbecue or an expedition to his
cottage the next weekend. One of us will have seen something in the paper that requires comment — that the rats
of Venice now outnumber people six to one, or that a
certain lawyer we both knew in school is running for
office or being sued for malpractice. Then after the children have been put to bed, hair wet and shining from
their baths, I will lock the doors and my wife and I will slip
between the sheets for a little action of our own, a glorious
symphonic crescendo after which we'll hold each other
and drift safe and weightless through our private universe.

Once, early on, Harold talked about his cancer, what
various books proposed as causes for this plague. I was
peeling carrots and throwing them into the juicer while
Harold worked on swallowing his shark cartilage pills. His
favourite theory, he explained between swallows, was that
cancer strikes your body when its defences are diverted by
stress — in other words, the nasty life its owner is living.

Translation: People get cancer because they weren't born rich, carefree, powered by inner certainty and peace. That was in his kitchen, a sunny day. Lots of room for sun because Harold wasn't taking up very much space. If his defences had been down before, now they had entirely disappeared. The next afternoon, driving in the country, he stopped to pee and his shadow was so thin he looked like a tree that had lost its leaves.

Amsterdam's canals. The small canvas-covered boats bobbing against the concrete walls, the fruit stalls on the bridges with red-eared vendors clapping their hands against the cold. The seventeenth-century buildings crowned by fantasy façades, the gruff voices of men calling to each other across crowded smoky pubs. The hotel where I was staying when Harold called to tell me he had cancer.

The telephone I crouched over, listening to my brother. The heavy glass-topped desk with its dark-red leather folder containing the room-service menu. The wall safe where I put my passport. The round marble coffee table. The bed where I collapsed.

The white-painted hand-hewn beams criss-crossing the ceiling. The tall brass lamp with its translucent gold-tinted glass column. The leaking shower. The way the cold creeps in, even through the handsomest of windows, the chill that installs itself in the bones of your feet, the constant rattle of passing bicycles, the impatient grunts and coughs of cars jockeying for parking spaces.

Eventually I went to the windows and looked out at the water. It was late October, the setting sun had soaked the sky in swirls of dark liquid red; as the colours rippled scenically on the water, birds swooped to feed from the surface, like some mystical poem about beauty, eternity, the perfect balance of life and death. But I didn't feel mystical, or consoled, or reassured by the crackle of life jumping up from the stillness. All I saw was so much blood-coloured water and hungry birds. When I telephoned Margaret with the news she cried sympathetically, tried to console, but nothing she offered could touch me. Only the children's voices could raise a spark. Only they were uncorrupted by the sudden ugliness death had splashed over the rest of us.

2

Some days I am in luck, and those children's voices come my way. I might be sitting in the kitchen armchair drinking a beer when Simon — while pacing the floor and devouring fourteen pieces of toast with peanut butter — decides to favour me with imaginary episodes of his favourite television shows, each graphically acted out complete with dramatic collapses on the floor, full-body ricochets off the refrigerator and cupboards, peanut-butter-spotted cries of triumph and agony. Weekend afternoons Emily likes to announce that I need a nap. Once she has me stretched out on the bed, she lies down beside me, holds a book above her face and reads King Arthur legends aloud. Knowing how squeamish I am, she warns me to close my eyes whenever the action is about to get violent; to further protect me she reads those passages as quickly as possible, without expression, so I won't get too frightened.

As I need their voices, they need mine. Every night my job is to tell them a story. For years these long continuing sagas featured the heart-rending adventures of a schizophrenic pig. Now a dog called Pinky had taken centre stage. Pinky also had problems — perhaps uncoincidentally the storyteller's problem — he is both terrified by and attracted to the sound of his own bark. Once he starts, panic sets in, and he barks at his own barking. Louder and louder he gets, trying, with each volley of barks, to drown out the previous. This vicious cycle escalates until he collapses with acute laryngitis and a sore throat. Finally, when Pinky is teetering on the very precipice of death, his mother takes him to Dr. Nunes-Dog for treatment. The world's foremost dog-metaphysician, Dr. Nunes-Dog concocts a pill to make Pinky's tongue swell up and taste like brussels sprouts at the very first bark.

It works! Finally Pinky is able to lead a normal life. He has gone back to being a star baseball player and now — yes — it's PINKY IN LOVE as the dog journals proclaim. There are pictures of Pinky emerging from limousines, his muzzle bound with silk scarves. Only Pinky knows the terrible secret of his silence, the awful consequences that could follow if . . . And that is where I ended tonight's chapter.

"So short," Emily complained when I told her the story was over, "Why was it so short?" The truth was that it was Emily's bedtime and I wanted to get to my office, my hidden bottles of Scotch, contemplate my options from

1 to Etc. What I said to Emily was that I was leaving out the boring parts. "There are no boring parts!" she protested. "If you don't tell the whole thing you wreck it!"

So. Option Whole Thing: What happened between Harold and me after he left me at the airport? A year and a half of total silence. During this time my mother, along with her reports of life as a museum lady, would send news of Harold's various promotions, raises, even a copywriting award — but from Harold himself, nothing. And vice versa. When I thought or spoke of Harold my mouth would go a certain way, a way it has shaped itself even now, writing this, a turned-down wounded shape that tugs sadly at the lips and the heart. I would think about what he had done to me, to Francine's baby, to me and Francine — then my mouth would turn down further and I would picture Harold waving goodbye to me at the airport. *Goodbye.*

It was Harold who broke the silence. Over the telephone his voice was warm and full of energy, uncomplicated by the slightest shadow. My mouth was trying to twitch doubtfully, but my traitorous heart melted right away and soon I was burbling with enthusiasm. I was in Paris for a month, exchanging places with a student I'd met at a conference. Harold was coming to London on a business trip and —

A few days later Harold appeared at the door. For the first time, I saw him in what was to become his trademark black Italian-suit costume. It made him look tall and polished, a sophisticated representative of a glamorous world I'd only previously seen on billboards and in magazines. Along with the suit he wore a flashy tie and his wide cock-eyed smile. In one hand he had a bottle of wine, in the other, flowers.

My borrowed apartment on the Rue St. Sulpice consisted of one small room plus a closet-sized bathroom. I fussed over dinner, which was pan-fried sole with lemon — following a real recipe from a French cookbook — accompanied by boiled new potatoes, string beans eviscerated French-style and a bottle of Sancerre. A feast! Unfortunately, each dish was only an approximation of its ideal and during dinner I kept leaping up to wash plates so they would be clean for the next course. Dessert was cheese, pears and the red wine Harold had brought. By the time we were sipping Harold's wine I was exhausted from jumping up and down and Harold had grown irritated watching me. When the sound of his fingers tapping began to drown out the traffic, I suggested we go out for coffee.

Playing the tour guide I took him up the Rue du Tournon towards the Senate and the Luxembourg Gardens. Part way I stopped, then dramatically pushed open a set of wooden gates wide enough to accommodate a horse-drawn carriage. It was a late summer evening, the courtyard was filled with a blue-purple glow. I pointed up to an unlit window. "Joseph Roth lived there," I announced emphatically.

Joseph Roth, as I'd told Harold at dinner, was one of the dead men of Europe I was trying to pin to the pages of the thesis I still believed I was writing, the thesis that would be the ticket to the life of scholarship and contemplation I still believed I would live as soon as, like a Kafka hero, I woke up transformed from my current unscholarly, uncontemplative, inconvenient being into a rational and ambitious cockroach.

At the end of the Rue du Tournon was the café where during the 1930s, I explained to Harold, Roth drank himself to death. My plan was that we join his ghost and I would amuse Harold with irresistible anecdotes about this brilliant alcoholic and his brilliant circle of fellow drinkers, unpredictable mistresses, scoundrels and bene-factors — most of whom, like Roth, had fled the rising fascist tides of the thirties to find refuge in Paris. And with a stained but irresistible smile, Paris had welcomed them into her cheap bistros and rickety hotels. Later, alas, she betrayed them — but that's life, I had decided to think; those who will betray you first open their arms. When we arrived at the café I was able to show Harold the plaque on which Joseph Roth's name had been inscribed but, unfor-tunately, the café was closed and we had to go take our coffee at a nearby McDonald's.

While we sat beneath the golden arches and Harold smoked a few cigarettes, I told him about Roth's daily visits to the café, that closed and unavailable café. The owner/bartender admired Roth so much that she agreed to reward each line he wrote with a glass of whisky. As I talk-ed, ever more nervous — this was possibly where I began to suspect that I should leave out the boring parts — Harold's fingers threatened to drum right through the table. He could rein them in while lighting a new ciga-rette, but then off they'd go — trot, canter, gallop. To en-courage them I began detailing even more of my exciting discoveries about Joseph Roth. Luckily I had just come across a fascinating book of letters between Roth and his Dutch publisher, and I already seemed able to recite them from memory. Harold yanked his galloping fingers off the table and dug his fists into his sleepy eyes. To increase the drama I told him about the dutiful young secretary to whom Roth — lying piteously in his sickbed — had dictated these letters.

Harold perked up. "When was that?"

"Nineteen-thirty-seven."

"You should find her," he said.

That was Harold. Ever the man of action.

The morning after the disastrous dinner, I passed a hat shop while walking towards Harold's hotel. Herr Meyser was on display. I went inside, thinking to buy the hat for myself. When I saw the price tag I started to retreat — but the owner insisted I try him on. Herr Meyser was far too large for me. But as I stood in front of the mirror, admiring the elegant bite of Herr Meyser's brim, I realized I could give him to Harold as an act of atonement.

Standing in his hotel room, unwilling to apologize and also afraid to open my mouth lest I begin speaking in paragraphs, I just said, "Here" and handed Harold the gift-wrapped hatbox.

"What's this stupid thing?" I half-expected Harold to blurt out. "Joseph Roth's hat? Where's the free drinks?"

But Harold received Herr Meyser with great ceremony. He held him, caressed him, set him on his head with the gentle appreciation of a connoisseur. When we went outside to walk, Herr Meyser sailed through Paris, confidently perched on Harold's large head, an emperor gracefully gliding through the streets of his imperial capital.

"This is better," Harold said. We were sitting on a *quai*, watching the sluggish flow of the Seine. It was late morning, the sky a trademark milky blue.

Harold lit a cigarette, but to my eyes he still looked vaguely disgruntled. In this noon light I could see Harold's face was growing heavier, weighed down by a fatigue I'd never before noticed.

"Do you still play basketball?" I asked.

"Is the Pope Jewish?"

"Barbecue?"

"Oh yeah. We got barbecues."

"We?"

Harold shook his head, then took off Herr Meyser and peered into the lining. "The royal we," Harold said.

We started walking again. At least he's come here, I said to myself, that must mean something. After a while Harold suggested we have lunch. "My treat," Harold said. He speeded up, his nostrils flared, Herr Meyser swivelled back and forth as Harold searched for just the right place. Finally he settled on an elegant and intimidating restaurant with its name posted in fine handwriting, linen tablecloths and vases of mortal flowers. On my own I would never have dared set foot in such a place. Harold, full of confidence, pushed open the door, shook hands with the maitre d' and, as soon as we were seated, demanded the wine list which he began to scan like the face of an old friend.

Soon we were eating a fabulous meal, washed down by exotic wines. Harold was smiling broadly, telling jokes, smoking between courses, smacking his lips. He had the waiters charmed and then he started a conversation with two women at the next table. It turned out they were Belgian airline stewardesses. When Harold told them we were brothers they were amazed. "But you're French!" one of them exclaimed. "And your brother is American!"

"Like our parents," Harold explained. "Our mother comes from a family of vintners in the Loire, but our father is a New York banker."

There was a bottle of champagne in honour of the château, now owned by thieves, then coffee with numerous brandies.

That night we met them again for dinner in a restaurant near the Eiffel Tower. Harold was expansive. Harold paid. Harold commandeered a taxi and took us to a right-bank nightclub where we listened to American jazz and drank bad Scotch.

After we parted from the stewardesses in the middle of the night, I asked Harold how he could afford to live this way.

"Expense account," Harold said. "When I get home, I'm quitting." I felt soaked but not exactly drunk. We began to walk. Except for the occasional taxi or police car, the streets were deserted. We came to the Rue de Rivoli. Harold stopped to look in the window of a men's clothing store. *Expense account*. The words had somehow stuck in my mind. The suits my parents had bought me were hanging unused in my Amsterdam closet. I was wearing an old jacket and a pair of jeans with which I had become particularly friendly. Harold, on the other hand — Harold. I hadn't, I realized, really *noticed* Harold. He was not only wearing his Italian suit, but his shoes had a dark happy glow, as though they'd been the ones knocking back the ten-year-old burgundy, and the gold frames of his glasses glinted in the streetlights. Harold was, as I'd told my father, *coining it* — Harold was loaded — Harold was, practically and literally, coated in money.

"What do you do with it?" I asked Harold.

"What?"

"All that money?"

"What money?"

"Look at you."

Harold opened his arms wide, looked down at himself. Then he clapped me on the shoulder. "You should have been a priest," he said. "I could get you a hair shirt for Hannukah."

We started walking again. Eventually we came to the Pont Neuf. One day it, too, would be wrapped in gold, but in the midst of this particular night it was surrounded by drifting strands of fog, a deep hollow silence. We stood, looking out at the river. The first night I'd been the one trying to impress. The second had been Harold's chance to dazzle. Now that we'd each had our turn, it was time to talk. To talk about Francine. We'd say what had to be said, the sliver would be drawn.

I was watching a certain bit of fog, it was shaped like a jagged cigar and luminous with the light it had trapped

from a streetlamp. It was slowly floating down the river.
I decided that when it had passed the streetlamp I would
ask Harold about Francine.

As I turned to Harold, he turned to me. He was looking
at me, but also through me. His face was stony, his eyes
half-closed. As though for him I, too, was just a temporary
bit of fog, a random assembly of moisture that had somehow briefly caught the light. Then he started walking again.

It was two more years before I returned to Canada. Instead
of moving back to Toronto, I decided to live outside the
city. That was when I found the farm. Long since abandoned by the giants who had carved it out of swamp and
rock, rendered worthless by encroaching brush, hyperactive beavers and global agribusiness, the one-time farm
had evolved into a glorious anarchy of mixed bush, wild
apple trees, and pine-surrounded ponds. What had once
been a one-room cabin was now four unconvincing walls
topped by a rotting shake-shingled roof and propped onto
a collapsing foundation.

During my time in Amsterdam a former member of the
Toronto Meyser cult, Elaine Jaeger, had become an editor
at a Toronto publishing house. Elaine offered me a job
ghost-writing the naughty memoirs of a prominent politician. Using my advance I made a down payment on the
farm and arranged for electricity to be brought in. After
installing myself, I tried to get the cabin ready for winter.

Every week I would drive to Toronto for a day of inter-
views with the politician. Following one of these sessions I
went for a beer at Elaine's. She and a friend were sitting on

the back porch of Elaine's ground-floor apartment, feet up on the railing, watching the cat stalk birds in the garden. Margaret's feet: small, strong, tough-skinned with short supple toes that could pick up a newspaper. And her eyes: dark, melting, brown-black eyes, slow-moving lingering eyes that, as the evening progressed, seemed to be lingering on me. A month later I met her again, again by chance. Then, one morning on the way into Toronto, I stopped at a gas station, phoned Margaret at her job and asked her to lunch. Her scent. The way her eyes stayed on mine until I, nervous, wavered. She had a heart-shaped face, creamy white skin, a long elegant neck and throat disappearing into a maroon silk blouse. She said, or at least I thought she said, "You can unbutton my blouse if you want to."

We were kneeling on the floor of her apartment, picking up the sugar cubes I had spastically dumped in my nervousness at being there.

I wanted to. The light spilling in the windows gave Margaret's face a bridal glow. She had invited me to unbutton her blouse but it seemed to me the invitation was an open one, no hurry was necessary, so I settled into staring at her face while she stared at mine. I was thinking about a novel I'd read in which the hero felt he was too old and ruined ever to fall truly in love again, if indeed the loves he had previously fallen into were true and not simply potholes of loneliness. On the other hand, the hand that should have been occupying itself with Margaret's blouse — but maybe she hadn't said "You can unbutton my blouse"; maybe she had said "You can look around the house."

I remained kneeling on the floor for a long time. My legs began to get sore. I couldn't hear Margaret's invitation any more, only its receding echo. Then Margaret herself receded. She stood up and asked if I minded if she played the cello. She stepped from the living room to the music room, which was the same room except that it was the part centred by a plain yellow oak chair, a cello upright in its open case, a metal stand holding a sheaf of sheet music.

As Margaret arranged herself, I walked the length of her small apartment, from the living/music room to the kitchen, which looked out to the spreading branches of a maple tree.

I missed the exact instant when Margaret started playing. By the time I was aware of myself listening, the smooth soft tones had already crept through the room, soaked the air, taken possession of me.

I went into the hall to be closer to the music. Stripped of its orchestra the cello sounded oddly bold and naked. But Margaret's music was so sad. As sad as Francine's mouth as she was being carried away on the stretcher. Each long drawn note was a low sigh full of sorrow, a dark-bellied cloud aching to break open. I lay down on Margaret's bed. Soon I could hear little bursts of fire rising through the sadness, lightning trills making unexpected circles above the darkness. When Margaret came in I was still floating on the music. We lay on her bed, rolled into each other, our breathing getting used to being two. Eventually I realized we were on a boat, together we had set sail. We were so fragile, the boat so small, our bodies our only refuge against the night.

It was March when I first showed Margaret the cabin. The hydro pole was lying on the ground, as it had been since they brought it in the fall and explained that the earth was frozen too deep for the pole to be raised and the wires connected.

I had warned Margaret that my cabin was primitive, but she may not have been prepared for the sight of a hydro pole lying wireless in the snow. We went in and lit the stove, a wood-hungry relic with a soot-covered mica window. When the fire was going I encouraged her to sit close enough to singe her jeans, and then opened the peach brandy I kept as a secondary heat source.

The next day the sun came out and the cabin warmed, but we were outside, walking and driving the muddy roads. I needed Margaret's eye on everything I had been looking at all winter. I needed her to walk back with me through the woods to the pond where I'd skied when it was minus thirty and the only way I could get warm in the morning was to light a fire and go skiing while the water in the kettle thawed so I could make coffee. I needed to show her the pine woods, the river that ran all winter long, my lucky twin oak trees. I needed her to help carry wood to the cabin from the unlucky trees I was chainsawing until my hydro pole could stand itself up and get itself connected to the nearest nuclear facility. Margaret trudged dutifully through the snow, lengths of elm and ash piled high in her arms. Then Margaret wanted a rest. She wanted to go to town and be taken out for dinner and a bottle of red wine. Amazingly, she wanted me.

When I told Harold about Margaret, he was relieved to have the explanation of why I no longer slept in his television room when I came to town. Their first meeting was on neutral ground, a restaurant. As we sat down I could see Harold surveying Margaret to see which camp she fell into — i.e., the helpless or the other. I had told him she was a cello player and no doubt he'd assumed the worst, but Margaret has mastered the external appearance of total competence. Harold being the same way, they got along famously. There was no nervous finger-drumming as we hit the second bottle of wine, and soon after, our cheeks burning and flushed, Harold explained to Margaret that her attendance would be required at a barbecue to be held that weekend — did she know that he was famous for his grilled artichokes? — and that she and I would be responsible for bringing a decent bottle of brandy and a salad.

As he said the word "brandy" Harold raised his hand. There was a final toast, a slight staggering as we made our way from the table into the cool outside air, the roar of Harold's latest red car accelerating into the darkness.

"Barbecue night at Harold's is an institution," I warn Margaret. I'm not sure if she's impressed but she spends the day before preparing a spiced shrimp salad in a bowl big enough to fill the circle of her arms.

When we arrive, Harold meets us at the door. A woman appears at his side, Harold's "vice-president in charge of everything". Her name is Nancy Prescott. "Like the highway," Nancy says when Harold introduces us. She looks at me carefully as she shakes my hand. There is something reserved and calm about Nancy, a quiet certainty that makes me feel good about her, about her and Harold, the easy way he is with her.

We are standing talking when we hear the sound of a baby starting to cry. "That would be Jake," Harold says. Nancy goes in to fetch him and before I can ask any questions others have claimed Harold's attention.

Harold has a small high-fenced yard that soon fills up with the usual crowd. Margaret ends up in a corner, talking to Nancy who now has Jake on her lap. Meanwhile Harold's dog is following me around, attracted by the brotherly smell.

I decide to confuse the dog further by giving him one of the cookies Harold likes to toss him. I lead him into the kitchen. Two men are leaning against the stove, drinking beer and arguing about the forthcoming election. One of them, an old basketball pal of Harold's, is familiar. We say hello, shake hands. The other, Jack, is new to me. He's big. He's wearing slacks and a "casual" shirt which makes him stand out among all the other men, dressed in old T-shirts, jeans and cut-offs. But he has powerful hands and forearm muscles that ripple with every movement: the arms, I can't help thinking, of someone who strangles people for a living.

It turns out he is, or is pretending to be, a Bay Street lawyer. One of Harold's clients, I warn myself, and instead of starting an argument I offer him another beer.

Later, standing in the garden with Harold, I ask him about the killer in the kitchen.

"Jack," Harold says.

"A big-time spender?"

"Nancy's husband," Harold says as Nancy approaches us, and loops her hand through Harold's arm.

The next afternoon in the gym. Harold and I alone. Harold laughing as I, out of practice after my years away, miss a series of easy shots. Harold leaping into a shaft of light. Twisting, lofting the ball with his old grace. The sound of leather on string. That's what brings it back to me. Harold and I alone in the afternoon light. The slap of leather against skin, the hollow sound of our feet on the hardwood floor. The soft perfect angles of the backboard. The easy floating glides, mid-air invention. Then standing in the shower, exhausted, blinded by steam, everything back.

"Who's this Nancy?" I ask.

Harold steps out of the shower without turning it off.

"Nancy?"

"Prescott. Like the highway."

"That's who," Harold says. He takes my shampoo and puts his head back under the water. I am still curious but a little warning sign labelled FRANCINE floats through my mind.

Later I ask Margaret what she thought of Harold, his party, his friends. I can hear the uncertainty in my own voice.

"Nice," Margaret says diplomatically.

"Nice."

"An interesting man," Margaret says.

The clock reads 4:45 a.m. I stand up and stretch. My eyes hurt and my back is sore. I've been so busy typing I've forgotten to drink my Scotch. I carry it with me up to the kitchen. As always my eyes go to the bulletin board, where Harold's obituary has been pinned for over four months. It is strange to read the obituary of someone you knew well, someone you've watched die, someone you've loved. Even pinning it to the bulletin board doesn't help.

> CONSTANTINE, **Harold,** at his home on August 3rd, 1992 in his 37th year, beloved son of Laura and the late William Constantine, dear brother of Alec. Sadly missed by friends and associates. Harold was a founder and patron of the Northern Juvenile Basketball League, Vice Chairman of the United Way 1988–1991, active with Big Brother and numerous other benevolent organizations. Remembrances to a charity of choice. The funeral —

The paper has started to turn yellow and curl at the corners. For the first time it occurs to me that I can't just leave it there, pinned for eternity like some rare dead butterfly.

I fill the kitchen window bird-feeder, pour the remaining Scotch down the sink, go upstairs. The only light still shining is the bathroom night-light. Walking carefully, trying to avoid the boards that creak, I feel spooked, the way I did that first night after I saw Harold at Club Elvis.

At the top of the stairs I pause to take off my clothes. When I've got them folded in a neat little pile over my arm, ready to deposit silently at the end of the bed — will my obituary include this thoughtful habit? — I stop and listen. There is something too vulnerable about standing naked in the hall of my own house, my toes gripping the paint, clothes clutched to my belly. Then I hear an unexpected sound — a low voice has spoken my name. Harold is somewhere in the house. A cupboard. A dark corner of the hall. Hiding ghostily under a bed or calmly sitting on the couch, waiting for me to find him. I whisper his name. Emily and Margaret both stir in their beds. Now I'm wide awake, heart pounding. Still standing on the top of the stairs, I put my clothes back on. Then I go down to the living room.

Light from a streetlamp seeps through the stained-glass windows above the curtains. The menorah — tonight was the second night of Hannukah — glows dully. A few hours ago Simon was proudly holding the lit match to the candles, repeating the blessing after me. *Baruch atah adonai* — the words come automatically. Then I hear the noise again. Not exactly a noise. A something. My heart accelerates. I go into the kitchen and snap on the light. Harold is sitting at the kitchen table.

"Alec. Did I wake you up?" There's a quickly melting trace of snow across the shoulders of his dark suit. He's looking frail but somehow hard. Rake-thin, narrow-faced, he is a steel-tempered version of himself, not the old Harold but the Harold who would logically have emerged — refined by his trial by fire — from the other side of his illness. His hair is greyer than it was at Club Elvis, and brushed straight back, but his bushy moustache is still black, still irrepressibly curved into a grin.

I sit down opposite him. Breathing is not so easy.

"Afraid?" Harold asks.

"Yes."

"So am I." His voice breaks, the way it did when he called me at the hotel.

Where it breaks, I fall through. There is nothing left in me to resist. I just hang on, breathing along with Harold, condemned. "Do you want a coffee?" I finally ask. Harold nods. I fill the machine, careful to be quiet, put an extra spoon of coffee in the filter basket so it will be strong, the way Harold likes it. Then I sit down again.

"I'm sorry," Harold says.

"It's not your fault."

Harold laughs. There is a bitter note in his laugh and I know if I go along with him I'll have that melt-down feeling, that warm sensation of being swept into the current of Harold and Harold's strange river.

"Why did you leave?" Harold asks.

"That morning on the beach? You're the one who left. I went to get coffee and when I came back —"

"That day. Any day . . ." This time he doesn't laugh, bitterly or otherwise. I know the days he means. The days and the nights. The times I couldn't bear his pain. But he couldn't bear it either, and he also couldn't leave.

"I wish I could have been better when you were sick," I say. "I should have been. I wanted to be. I just couldn't —"

My throat feels like it did at the funeral, knotted with razor blades and distress. I want to cry. But Harold is the one who is dead. Or not dead. I want to laugh with how crazy this is but my throat hurts too much.

"You did your best," Harold finally says, his voice softer. "You tried. I know it was hard for you."

"Your best was so good," I say to Harold. "You were —" I interrupt myself. "You were a saint."

"A *saint*," Harold repeats. Harold is sitting up tall, suddenly the kitchen walls are shrinking around us. "You're such a bastard, Alec, did anyone ever tell you that? A saint, *Christ*, I never wanted to be a saint. I wanted to be *alive!*" He laughs at me, mocking, and as he does his voice grows loud and angry, filling the room. Now the house can't contain Harold, the floors and walls are shaking. I wait, terrified, for Margaret and the children to come running downstairs.

Harold's face is scarlet, his fists clenched. "I *needed* you!" He screams. Harold's furies have finally found their own sledgehammer, raised it high, smashed it down in vengeance. He is leaning towards me, eyes burning, his hands now spread wide, fingers flexing and grasping for what only Harold can see.

My heart, laid bare, locks. For a moment, or for ever. Then gradually the echo retreats and the wild black cave of Harold's mouth shrinks back into a mustachioed smile. The coffee machine goes into its final spluttering convulsions. Harold looks up at the bulletin board, sees his obituary.

"So there it is," he says pleasantly. He reads it over while drinking his coffee. Then he puts his cup down and goes to the front door. "See you later," he says. He walks out the door and starts down the street. The newspaper has already arrived. CHRISTMAS FOOD BANK CRISIS the headline advises. I take the paper back to the kitchen. The microwave reads 5:31. On the floor, beneath the chair where Harold was sitting, are two small puddles of melted snow. I begin going through the cupboards for tuna and boxes of rice.

3

After the New Year, classes resumed. There was something soothing about my students, bright irresistible puppies secure in their dream of life. Although they had their own problems. In fact most seemed to be on medication — legal or otherwise — and well-provided with doctors' notes to explain late assignments. These notes I always accepted without hesitation. On the official form I would write: *Extension granted. Incomplete because of illness.*

When I wrote the word "illness", I thought about myself. Lately, I had progressed from reading obituaries to the "Life" section. It began with the astrology column — since I had apparently entered the world of the occult I thought it might have special messages for me. When it invited me to "Enjoy a romantic evening", I would go shopping at the market, then spend the afternoon cooking dinner. If it said, "You should be sensitive to the needs of your family", I would do Emily's homework with her, or take Simon over to the gym to play basketball. Sometimes, watching Simon abandon gravity as he leapt towards the basket, I would have various consoling thoughts about the continuity of life, completing the circle, etc. Feeling stronger, I branched out from the horoscope to columns about fashions and psyches. Finally I sank into those long worrying articles about that "illness" called "depression". Illness, as in my recovery from Harold's death. Illness, as in *Extension granted. Incomplete because of illness.*

One day, while reading about "Life", I came upon an article about marriage. According to the writer, not pictured but tantalizingly described as "the eminent Toronto psychoanalyst, Dr. Maria Julian", marriages often collapse because the partners fail to communicate. "Everyone worries about sex," Dr. Julian noted, "but then they neglect even more elementary forms of communication. For example, how often do exhausted spouses take the time to really look at each other? To do something as easy as calling each other on the telephone?"

Exhausted spouses. That rang a bell I'd already started to hear. In Margaret's strained voice. The tired way she hauled herself up and down the stairs. My own mumbled late-evening declarations that I was going down to my office to "do some typing". Never, since Harold had fallen sick, had Margaret said "What about me?" But now, reading and re-reading Dr. Julian's wise words in the Life section, I realized fate was sending me a signal. It was time to renovate my marriage. I called Margaret at the office and asked her how she was. "Fine," she replied, puzzled.

"The meeting with the accountant isn't until tomorrow." Of course I'd forgotten, but Arts Council budget cuts were threatening the orchestra with bankruptcy. I confirmed the arrangements for picking up the children, then turned back to the article. "Many marriage partners forget the elementary courtesy of asking each other about his or her day."

That evening, after Pinky scored big points by taking this advice to heart, I came downstairs, sat opposite Margaret and repeated the magic formula.

"How was your day?" I inquired, as though Dr. Julian was watching us through a one-way mirror.

"Why do you ask?"

"I'm interested. Isn't it normal for me to be interested in your life?"

"It would be."

Eventually Margaret got used to it. Each night I'd pop the question and she would tell me what so-and-so was doing to so-and-so in the office. I'd think I was listening attentively, then discover myself in the kitchen, refilling my drink while she was still talking. When I'd get back she'd announce she was going upstairs for her bath.

One evening when I asked Margaret about her day she looked at me curiously, the way she sometimes inspected the children's lunch-boxes for uneaten carrots. "How about *your* day?"

"The usual," I said.

"What if you had to give it a mark? Was it an 'A' day? A 'B' day? A 'C' day?"

"Incomplete," I replied without thinking.

"Well," said Margaret, a sudden edge to her voice. "Maybe I can help you finish it off."

A pause.

"I came home early this afternoon," Margaret said.

"You did?"

"I did."

"Were you feeling sick?"

"No," Margaret said. Then she stood up. "I think I'll get a drink."

It was a January night. Like other January nights. The curtains had been closed for hours. Dinner was over, the dishes washed, the children in bed. Margaret came back into the living room and sat down. We each had our favourite places. Hers was a red velvet sofa long enough to turn sideways and stretch out her feet. Mine was a blue armchair. Beside my armchair was a little table where I liked to stack the books I was reading. In the old days, the days before Harold got sick, I would often inspect the stack as though it were a pile of delicious presents, eager to be consumed. Every week or two I would go to the bookstore to make sure it had new delights to offer. Now the table sagged beneath the same books that had been gathering dust for almost a year.

"Don't you want to know what I did?" Margaret asked when she returned. "You see, I *have* noticed how you've been making an effort lately. So I decided to do the same. I decided to buy a bottle of wine, come home, and try to get you to come to bed with me." Margaret was looking down at her glass, which was filled with Scotch, not wine, and her voice did not sound desperate to seduce.

"That was nice," I said.

"When I came in I didn't see you so I went down the basement to your office. Your agenda was spread out on your desk and I looked to see if I had your schedule wrong."

"I went to the gym. Thought it was time I got back in shape."

"I like your chair," she said.

"You gave it to me."

"Then I realized I've been thinking this whole time that you've been having an affair. So I turned on your computer and looked under the 'letters' directory."

"That one to the advice column was just a joke. I never sent it."

"Then I thought, well, of course you're not going to put your love letters where I can find them so easily; you're too paranoid for that, so I searched through the other directories and found that thing you're writing."

Margaret's eyes were glistening with the beginning of tears. She was squeezing her hands together. I crossed the room, I took her hands in mine. Why hadn't I stayed home? Why couldn't we be in bed, making up the way we knew how? Why couldn't we be anywhere but here, in the harsh light of the living room, Margaret's hands still twisting, her eyes refusing to meet mine.

"I never told you about Francine because . . . it was so long ago."

"So long ago? Come on, Alec, all those times you and Francine were at Harold's when he was sick? You must have had ten thousand chances. And now, well, *I was at the gym getting into shape*, Alec, I'm not an idiot."

"Margaret, that's crazy —"

"Don't call me crazy." She pulled her hands from mine. "But I believe you. Or I don't care. If you want to know the truth. You know what really bothers me? The way you see yourself as some kind of zero. A nothing with no connection to anyone. As if no one loved you and your life was just — something you make up."

Her knees were digging into my thigh. As her voice rose, I went dead inside, the way I'd felt when I called to tell her Harold was sick. She started to say something about self-respect.

"I love you," I said. I *did* love her, or at least I had loved her before, loved her, longed for her, felt with her a mysterious and necessary fullness that was even more than love. But my voice sounded unconvincing, even to myself. "The children," I invoked. "You can't say I don't love the children."

"You know how you write about yourself?" Margaret asked. Her knees jabbed harder and I had to keep myself from moving away. "Like someone I don't know. Not like a real person with a real life and family and job and friends but as though you don't care if you live or die. As though you're some kind of creature from outer space shrivelling up in the earth's atmosphere. You say you love the children. What kind of love are you giving them? Zombie love. You're off somewhere — Club Elvis, God knows where — you think it's such a tragedy that your brother died. Every hair, every finger, you dwell on it as though he were some kind of god. What do you suppose Simon and Emily are thinking about you? Don't they need you as much as you need Harold?"

Now Margaret was looking at me. Something had happened to her, I realized, not just this afternoon but over these past few months. Whatever I'd been doing to her was just as real to her as losing Harold was to me. But I felt nothing. I felt like stone. Then I knew that just as I had lost Harold I was now going to lose Margaret.

"I also liked the way you portrayed me. The meek little wife lying down, smiling and doing nothing while you're off fantasizing about Francine. All that stuff about the sun in my eyes, my perfect mouth. Was I supposed to be a person or a painting? I loved it. And who's the two-way Elvis supposed to be? Is he going to sing the lullabies while you and Francine waltz off into the sunset?"

I couldn't look at Margaret any more.

"I wish we'd never met," Margaret said in a bitter voice I didn't want to hear.

The living room had turned into a car. A dark ugly car speeding drunkenly out of control. We would survive the crash, but not together. And then Emily — Emily who never wakes up, was standing at the doorway of the living room, holding her stuffed dog and looking at us.

"I had a nightmare." She stepped in and sat on my lap. I wrapped my arms around her the way, when she was little, I used to hug her and tell her that I was never going to let her go and that she'd better arrange to have her meals delivered. She snuggled into me. STONE-HEARTED ADULTERER STOOPS TO USING CHILD AS HUMAN SHIELD.

Margaret crossed the room and knelt in front of Emily, stroking her hair. Soon Emily was draped over my shoulder, being carted up to bed, while with her hands she clung to Margaret, following close behind. Necessary angels we hovered in her room, brooding over her while she settled back into sleep.

After her bath Margaret reappeared wearing her Extreme Cold nightgown, a flannelette chastity castle that covered her thickly from neck to ankles.

That night I began sleeping in the basement. When the children came down to watch television I explained that I had to sleep on the floor because I'd hurt my back playing squash. "You don't know how to play squash," Simon pointed out cleverly. "That's right, Daddy," Emily cried, jumping on me enthusiastically. "That's why I hurt myself," I said. "Now you've injured me again, I might have to lie on this floor for the rest of my life." That was part of a game we used to play, the children and I, pretending crazy glue had stuck us into some absurd position, and the stuck person would be pulled and tugged by the unstuck people until they came loose. Now Emily just gave me a funny look and said, "Good."

4

The doctor's office is suspiciously located on a street of very fashionable boutiques. Her building houses a variety of professional healers — dentists, hair-replacement specialists, two past-lives therapists — and also features several offices apparently rented to fur and leather merchants. "Feature", I suddenly remember, was one of Harold's favourite words. "Tonight's feature will be grilled cheese, with a caesar trailer." Our key words — "feature", "speech", "parents", dozens more — had taken on their own meanings over the years and allowed us to communicate in shorthand, a private language I can still speak but will never again hear.

The doctor is the newspaper oracle herself, Maria Julian. It is time, I have realized, to move beyond the Life section to Life itself. "I have an appointment to see Dr. Julian," I announce to the secretary. I am carrying my briefcase and suddenly I feel like a drug salesman.

"The doctor," replies the secretary. In this office mere human names have been transcended. The secretary is the secretary, the doctor the doctor. Neither the secretary nor the doctor will think I am the salesman. They will think I am the patient. "The doctor" is late. "The doctor" has called to say she's on her way. "The doctor" needs to have these forms filled out. "The doctor" will see you now. The doctor has large glassy brown eyes. Ivory-coloured skin. A wide matronly body and an aggressive way of leaning towards me that makes her large glassy eyes bulge and threaten to roll right out of their sockets and bounce across the desk. No wonder her picture isn't in the newspaper.

The doctor asks if I would mind replying to a few questions. My plan is to explain I have come to be treated for the depression I have felt ever since the death of my brother, that although I have perhaps been depressed before, on other occasions, that never have I gone through something like this, with such a clear-cut cause, nor, since meeting Margaret and becoming a father and responsible member of society, have I ever become so depressed that I felt I was endangering my family, along with my position in it; never before have I been in a permanent state of semi-absence, never, in every sense, *incomplete because of illness*.

The doctor's first question concerns my medical insurance number, which I have already given to the secretary. I give it to the doctor and she writes it down with her gold fountain pen. Then she asks my date of birth followed by whether I was happy as a child.

This is my cue. "I liked my family," I say, "but now most of them are dead."

"Most of them are dead?"

"My brother and my father. Also a sister who died as an infant."

"But your mother is still alive?"

"Yes."

"That must be a consolation," the doctor offers, leaning forward. Her eyes bulge alarmingly, and I hold out my hands to catch them on the first bounce. The last thing I need is to spend the rest of my afternoon down on my knees with the doctor, crawling around her office looking for her eyes.

"After my brother died, my wife says I stayed drunk for several months."

"When did he die?"

"Several months ago."

"You have a drinking problem then?"

"Not really."

"Good."

She pulls her head back and her eyes settle into their sockets as she writes something on her pad. I wonder if I should tell her that my back is sore because the basement floor is so cold. But that would be digressing. I decide to stick to the subject.

"Also, since my brother died I've been feeling — I don't know —" I pause. This is it. I have opened the door. Now the doctor should walk in and cure me. I used to have the same feeling waiting for a needle.

"Were you and your brother close?"

"Very." But if Harold and I were so close why hadn't we talked more — about Harold's dying, about the fact that our brotherhood was headed for the wall. Had I been the one dying, I would have talked about it all the time. People would have gotten sick of it. I would have complained constantly, accused Margaret of having affairs, my children of being repelled by me — there was no end to the unpleasant things I would have said and thought if I were dying. One day I *will* be dying and, though Harold has set a good example, it will be hard for me to follow.

"What are you thinking now?"

"How horrible I would be if I were dying."

"You are dying."

"Not today," I say hopefully. The open door is starting to close. Sometimes when students talk to me about their writing I can see their doors open and close. I never want to go in those open doors. Nor do I want to give them needles or any other kind of cure. I just hope that one day when the door is open whatever they need will come to them. Then the aspiring writers can become actual writers and trade the joyful optimism of wanting to be a writer for the repetitive misery of being one.

"What are you thinking?" the doctor asks.

"That writers are miserable. I'm a writer."

"What do you write?"

"Books." I hate it when people ask what I write. If I were a nail-cutter would people ask if I do toes or fingers? "Two novels. Sometimes short stories. Magazine articles. Television plays."

"I thought I might have seen you."

"I just write the lines."

"Maybe you were on television for something else."

"I have been," I say.

"So have I," says the doctor. Her jaw muscles go slack, she puts down her pen and her eyes recede fully into their sockets.

"There is one other thing."

"It's your nickel," the doctor says.

"After my brother died I started seeing him again."

"Don't worry about that. It's entirely normal. Many people have had such experiences, I assure you; it's nothing to be anxious about."

"I know what you mean, but this is different. I *really* saw him. A couple of times in a nightclub. I even talked to him. Then the other night he showed up in my kitchen."

"Were you afraid?"

"Yes."

"Good. It's normal to be afraid in such circumstances. I had a client, you would know her name, she's also in television, her dead husband joined her in the jacuzzi with her new lover. *That* was a problem. The important thing is to communicate."

We sit in silence for a moment while I absorb this advice.

"Thank you for coming," the doctor says. "I think we've made a good start."

Outside the sun had set. A few snowflakes were blowing out of the grey-yellow sky, a cold wind attacked my neck and ears. I headed for a Bloor Street bar that was always deserted at this time of day. It is the only bar in Toronto where the barman actually knows me. His name is Arthur Lipton, and he plays handball at the same gym where Harold and I used to shoot baskets. Once I introduced Arthur to Harold and the three of us, modestly wrapped in our white towels, conversed for a few minutes in the locker room.

After ordering a double Scotch with a beer on the side — fortunately I have no drinking problem so am allowed this — I opened my briefcase and pulled out *The Death of Faustus*, the new Dr. Meyser book I was supposed to be reviewing. His first book, the one that had drawn me to Amsterdam — *White Men Dying* — had been full of disparate quotations juxtaposed, wild and extravagant theories about everything from Freud's cigar to evolution's failure to give male humans a future. Faustus had died, according to Dr. Meyser, when people stopped believing in good and

evil. The great nineteenth-century heroes, from the stumbling giants in black to the ridiculous white-coated would-
be lovers and television stars, always achieved success by
making the Faustian bargain. But now we can no longer
bargain with the Devil because we believe neither in him
nor the soul he might like to purchase. How can you trade
away eternal life when you've killed the Messiah with
washing machines and cable television?

Such weighty thoughts demanded another round. The
truth is, I've always been convinced that — given the
chance — I would be glad to sell my soul if only I had the
guarantee of a perfect book. Or even nearly perfect. But
the Devil has never offered; perhaps Dr. Meyser was right
— the Devil has failed to appear because I have failed to
believe. Harold on the other hand, Harold *had* appeared.

I looked at my watch. Somehow it had gotten to be
seven o'clock. By now they would have eaten supper. Margaret would be angry at me for being late. The prospect of
going home and facing Margaret's silent hostility, the
puzzled reproachful looks from the children, the chilly
basement floor, the continuous rattle of the furnace, was
not attractive. "Who'd want that?" I said.

"Not me," Arthur replied. He was standing beside my
table. "How's the writing?"

"Not bad." I don't mind Arthur asking me about my
writing. If he wanted to know, I would even tell him about
my books, including those in which he appears — always
as an attractive character.

"Slow?"

"Stuck."

"Maybe you need to write on napkins," Arthur suggested. "Ernest Hemingway always wrote on napkins when he drank here."

"When Ernest Hemingway lived in Toronto, this place didn't exist."

"Don't be so sure. He always drank gimlets with pickled onions. My mother used to pickle the onions."

"Did you box with him?"

Arthur rubbed his stomach easily. He has been blessed with a substantial stomach. Then he gave me one of his patented Arthur smiles, the slow considered smile of a man in a high-powered launch, a man on permanent vacation, a man who has solved his own personal puzzle, hung it on the wall, and is now free to pursue small amusements.

"No, he never did ask me to box. But one time he asked me to dance."

"That's not much of a punchline," I complained, but Arthur stood his ground, rubbing his stomach. He placed several paper napkins on the table.

"Try them out. Maybe they're lucky."

Dear Harold, I wrote.

> Tell me you love me
> Tell me you care
> Tell me who
> You are and where

I looked at the words I had written. They didn't fill up much napkin, but they were my whole message.

I drank a final Scotch, this time accompanied by coffee. On my way out I stopped in the bathroom. My face looked pale and wintry, exhausted from hanging on to something it could neither possess nor let go.

Outside the weather had warmed and the snow was falling thick and hard. The yellow glimmers of light in the sky had been succeeded by the bright headlights of cars slowly cruising through the snowy streets. I dropped the napkin in a mailbox. Watching it disappear I had a beautiful feeling inside me, that golden glow I used to get after writing something utterly brilliant, utterly unrefusable. In the long ago days of my great genius, before I started teaching, in the days when I was securely at the centre of my dream, I loved to drop envelopes into mailboxes, listen to them clack or thud to rest with the certain knowledge that such a gift could never be refused. For weeks after I would smile whenever I thought of my masterpiece glistening in its envelope somewhere, or open and being admired on the desk of the editor of some great magazine or publishing house. After that, it seems, I gradually lost my taste for writing. Or the taste of writing itself changed. Who knows? Perhaps one day I will meet the doctor a second time — in the subway or the lobby of another psychiatrist or past-lives therapist. Maybe we'll both be dead. Maybe we will end up on our knees together looking for her eyes. Maybe she will ask me about the taste of this particular writing. I'll tell her it is altogether new, a bittersweet taste that mixes death and hope in ways I don't yet understand, a taste of early summer and wind through the pine trees, a taste of the sickroom, a taste of the Russian cigarettes Dr. Meyser used to affect when I first knew him, of Emily's cinnamon-scented breath, of Francine in the shower.

When I was almost home I realized that I was now unforgivably late. The remains of dinner would be in the refrigerator, congealing in a plastic box and the children would be getting ready for bed, having been told "Daddy is still at work" or some such explanation they aren't intended to believe. I needed hot food in my belly, something to counter the drinking and give me the strength to face what was coming. I stopped at a corner restaurant, had a greasy hamburger and fries washed down with several cups of coffee. Feeling worse but more sober, I then continued towards home.

The slow-falling snow had a pleasantly moist smell. Responsible citizens were out enjoying the break in the weather, shovelling their steps or walking their dogs. The streets were full of students, their knapsacks and toques layered with snow as they returned home from the library and evening classes. Like the other houses, my own had its outside light on, an orderly welcoming glow. As I approached, Margaret opened the door. She was looking out at the street and, finally, as I came to our walkway, she was looking at me. There was no smile, no softening, nothing but a glassy appraising look that made me stop where I was. She was standing in the doorway, rigid, the light a golden blanket falling over her. For a moment I thought she was about to come towards me. Her mouth twitched as though to speak. Perhaps I, also, was going to speak. Then, slowly and deliberately, Margaret shut the door.

WIFE SHUTS DOOR IN DADDY'S FACE. Despite the snow, my face, the face in which the door had been shut, began to burn. I had the keys in my hand, was squeezing them between my fingers, but my feet refused to move. Simon's light was on. Perhaps he would appear at the window, rescue me. Surely Margaret would come back and open the door, act as though nothing had happened. Or I would open it myself, and walk in radiating false cheer and the story of my encounter with sanity. The falling snow was melting on my glasses. Finally my feet started on their way. They were taking me towards the university. I could phone Margaret from my office, even stay the night there. I wouldn't be the first to use my office as a refuge from marital stress or even as a cocoon for an illicit honeymoon. Then my feet changed their mind and headed south towards Queen Street. Queen Street was thick with traffic moving at a crawl though the snow. The sidewalks, too, were crowded. Everyone was in a hurry, going somewhere, talking loudly, laughing. I drifted towards the lane where Club Elvis used to be. And is again.

Club Elvis — back with the dazzling fluorescent flash of a magician's long-lost scarf suddenly reappearing from the gaping mouth of the most astounded spectator — Club Elvis!

Appropriately impressed, I stand and I gawk and I stare. The sign is where it used to be but now the CLUB ELVIS letters have been electrified and bleed their loud scarlet message into the snowy night.

I am moving down the path towards the club door when a hand slips through my arm. "So. Here we are."

Again my face begins to burn, and I feel as though I have been caught in an infinitely embarrassing deception.

"Aren't you glad to see me?" Francine asks.

There is a coy note in her voice that makes me laugh. Francine laughs too. She is wearing a fuzzy little red cap that looks like it should be whirling around a skating rink, her eyes are carefully limned with black, she has on a dark coat out of some war movie in which the hero is travelling to certain death while the beautiful woman — who has betrayed him offscreen — pretends she is flirting. Her lips quiver, edge towards a smile. "Say something. Tell me what you're thinking."

We are standing in the snow, looking at Club Elvis while the sign makes the air throb red. The door opens; a boozy couple stumbles towards the street, their hands up against their faces to protect them from the cold.

"I am glad to see you," I say. "Surprised."

"Surprised?" And then Francine begins walking and I'm happy to be walking with her, striding down Queen Street. Soon we're in a hotel bar, our coats off. Francine is sitting on a banquette, I'm on a chair, leaning towards her. I think how wonderful it would be to simply excuse myself — from Francine, from life — and take a room in the hotel and sleep for a week.

Francine looks at me. Her eyes are like deep mysterious pools. "What are you thinking now?" she asks.

"Your eyes are like deep mysterious pools."

"That was nicely put," Francine says. "I'm going to write it my diary."

She bends down for her purse. Her golden hair is rich and burnished. I remember the smooth wet feel of it, its flowery fragrance, the cool weight of it on my chest. Francine pulls out a clothbound book with a small brass hasp, one of those diaries you can buy in drugstores to record your innermost thoughts, and lock with a key you wear next to your heart.

Francine's heart, or at least the beat of it, the beating of Francine's heart in the ribs below her left breast, the cool sweet skin closest to her heart, the way I listened to the beating of her heart, the way my tongue followed its pulse to her neck, her wrists, her ankles, a vein in her temple hidden by hair, her heart's pulse that was magnified inside her.

We are sitting across from each other. We are drinking Papaya Bellinis. The recipe is, Francine tells me, champagne, papaya juice, customer-supplied navel lint. She doesn't have any, so she has to borrow some from me. This is no problem — my main talent is the manufacture of navel lint. It's a trick, I tell Francine, that I learned in the navy. I am so tired. I can't drink any more. Francine is looking at me, the deep mysterious pools of her eyes filled with concern. This, it occurs to me, is the first time Francine has ever really looked *at* me, not through or around or off to one side. Her eyes open wider.

I look into Francine's eyes. I am suspended above Francine, the hotel room is dark, waves of snow gust against the window. "Now tell me what you're thinking." Francine's skin so ghostly white. Francine's heat. Francine tastes like the seas of unnamed planets. Francine on my tongue, in my mouth, Francine filling me as I fill her.

Pleasure and pain. The pleasures of Francine. The pleasure of desire fulfilled. The pain of knowing this pleasure is cutting me away from Margaret. The pain of desire galloping beyond itself, beyond the merely human limitations of my merely human body, dragging me with it for the wild hurting ride until finally desire abandons us and we are left dizzy and exhausted in the hotel half-darkness of a snowy night. I am holding Francine's hand though at first I don't know it because our skin has melted together. And then finally I feel her fingers laced into mine and I remember the way it began with Margaret, the night we sailed into our uncertain future. We turn to each other and Francine offers me a smile, a smile you wouldn't think a devil could have, a smile tinged with sadness, resignation, but also a message that tells me I've touched her and that she's touched me — and wasn't that what I wanted all these years? To touch Francine and be touched by her?

The following afternoon I had two seminars to give. Part way through the second, a fourth-year workshop in which a student was giving a paper on "T.S. Eliot's Feminist Poetic", I realized I wasn't thinking about T.S. Eliot, feminism or even Francine. The face that was in my mind and wouldn't leave was Margaret's. When my class was over I rushed to my office. Still wearing my coat, I stood at my desk and began to punch out Margaret's number. But what was I going to say? I took off my coat. A student came in, needing me to explain why he had received a C⁺ on his most recent story. Seeing his grade reminded me of Margaret's question, the bitter note in her voice. Looking over his paper I wondered why I hadn't failed it. Another student arrived, one of my favourites because she allowed me to bum her cigarettes. When she left I locked the door. Then I took two pieces of paper and labelled them LIFE #1 and LIFE #2.

LIFE #1. All paths lead to Margaret and the children. In this life, my task is to climb the mountain. At the top is a rocking chair where I'll sit looking out at the clouds, surrounded by grandchildren and well-wishers, chuckling at the obvious serenity of it all. Of course, as I'll explain to the interviewers, it wasn't easy getting here. Often I couldn't even see where I was going. During those times I would fall prey to Digression, my chronic malady, stray from the path and find myself tripping over hurdles and falling into brambly elephant pits. In LIFE #1, an inspirational info-mercial in which hard work, virtue and a few forgiven idiocies lead to inevitable triumph, Harold is my tragic loss, Francine the great temptation I must give up. I desperately want to be in this LIFE #1, but have a terrible feeling someone else is going to get the part.

LIFE #2: This life has a script written by Dr. Meyser. In this life Harold and I are a dark double star. Francine was unwittingly pulled into our orbit and destroyed, along with her unborn child. Then Harold died, descended into purgatory taking Francine's soul with him. I am now following. In this LIFE #2, the Digression — really just a wishful hallucination — is not Harold but my years with Margaret and the children. But now Margaret has realized how evil I am and is struggling to save herself and the children. Forget Faust. I'm not bargaining with the Devil but with myself. If I have any decency at all, any shred of love for Margaret, Simon and Emily, I must let them go, gracefully disappear from their lives before putting my metaphorical hat over my face and following Harold and Francine to the hell which is to become my eternal home.

I re-smoked my student's cigarette butts while reading over these two pages. By now it was dinner-time. I telephoned home.

"It's me," I said. "What's happening?"

"The children are at my sister's." Margaret's voice sounded comfortable.

"I'm sorry about last night but when you shut the door —"

"I know."

"Can I come over?"

"Of course. I was expecting you."

As I emerged from my office the streetlights were laying a festive sparkle over the newly fallen snow, the air was snappy and clear, a crescent of moon cut whitely through the bare branches. When I got to our house there was still a thin layer of snow crusted on our walk. I took the shovel, scraped it clean. What a citizen! What a householder! But no matter how hard I shovelled, my body and face still felt as they had in the middle of the night with Francine, torn open, rearranged, irreversibly transformed.

Margaret was sitting at the kitchen table, her arms crossed in front of her, reading the paper. Otherwise the table was bare, and the smell of cooking definitively absent. When Margaret looked up at me I could see her eyes were swollen.

"You look tired," I said.

"I am."

"Trouble sleeping?"

"I was packing."

I sat down. Margaret pushed her fingers through her hair, the way she used to when she'd been practising for so many hours that her shoulders hurt and a headache had started.

"Your things," Margaret elaborated. "Then I stopped. You can finish on the weekend. I'm going to New York. You pick up the kids from school Friday. I'll be back Sunday before midnight."

Inside, total panic, as though some gremlin with a chainsaw were running through my guts. "So what's the plan?"

"That's my plan. Yours is — I don't know. Maybe you want to find somewhere. If you don't, I will."

I went to the cupboard, took out the Scotch. "Want one?"

"Please," Margaret said.

She was wearing a navy blue cardigan with black half-round buttons. The black buttons matched her eyes, the navy blue set off her olive skin. Her sleeves were pushed up, the top buttons undone. One afternoon, only a few eons ago, we'd come home from work early, sat on our bed while I slowly undid those black leather buttons. The perfect whiteness of her brassiere. The small mole on her breast that I always used to kiss when I took it off.

"I don't want this," I said.

"I do. I need it."

I gave Margaret her usual mixture of Scotch and water. Me: much more Scotch, much less water. A big swallow and the chainsaw was at least temporarily slowed.

"We can talk next week, after I get back. Tonight you can just take what you need until the weekend."

"I'll use the old blue suitcase."

"I've already used it, for the kids' summer clothes. I was putting away their laundry and there was no room in their drawers."

For some reason, her saying this made me realize how serious she was. Margaret always did the laundry, but until today, I had always put it away.

I came around the table and stood behind Margaret, began massaging her shoulders. She sat still, neither accepting nor pushing me away. I stopped and went over to the refrigerator.

"Sorry about supper," Margaret said. "I took the children for pizza. You could phone them tomorrow night if you want. They're probably wondering what happened to you."

All the lights were on upstairs. I went into Simon's room. Remembered the night after I'd first seen Harold at

Club Elvis. Coming back to be with the children. Needing to see and hear them breathing in the night. Now Simon's lights were ablaze, his bed empty, his room a mess. Margaret had made it look as though Simon had disappeared for ever. Emily's room, too, was inside out, her stuffed toys on the floor, her T-shirts and shorts piled in mounds. I sat down on her bed. On the table her glass of water was half-drunk, there was a cup with the remains of an apple, and the smell of the apple mixed with Emily's smell provided a sudden round of high-octane fuel for the chainsaw gremlin.

Stuffed beneath our bed was the small suitcase I used when I had to go away for short trips or conferences. I put in a few things, then went into the bathroom for my razor and toothbrush. A big plastic bottle of antacid tablets sat on the corner of the sink. I helped myself to a handful and started chewing on them. What a great scene this would be: WRITER CHEWS ROLAIDS WHILE PACKING TO MOVE OUT OF OWN HOUSE.

Now Margaret was playing the cello. If I lay down on the bed would she come and cleave to me? No, she would ask me to leave. I didn't want to hear Margaret's small hard voice asking me to leave. I closed the door to our bedroom, gently at first, then suddenly with so much force that it slammed loudly and the doorknob broke.

Margaret played on.

I went downstairs. Margaret was in the dining room, sawing away as though the world weren't ending. I stood in the door for a moment. She looked up. We turned away from each other and I left.

6

1

YOU *were a saint,* Alec had said; you could hear his voice thickening as he laid it on. Harold looked across the room to Francine. She was wearing her Benjamin Franklin-style reading glasses with rectangular lenses and gold frames and was doing the crossword puzzle. Francine was a *fiend* for crossword puzzles. In her reading glasses she looked — well, she looked like an enormously serious and beautiful woman devoted to a task that was, above all, *intricate.* Yes, *intricate* was the word for Francine, thought Harold.

Then Francine said, "How about this? Eight letters meaning fitting closely."

"Intricate?"

"Maybe. No. It has nine."

Harold looked out the window. He saw a pigeon trying to peck at its own behind. "Dovetail?"

Francine raised her head. Every time she moved the light fell on her golden hair in a different way. "How did you get that?"

"I saw it outside."

"Let me try it." She pencilled in the letters. "Let me ask you something."

"If I'm so smart how come I'm dead?"

Francine laughed. Again she looked like an enormously serious and beautiful woman, but this time there was a new note in her laugh, the note of someone on the verge of gliding away. As she left, Harold thought, his farewell line could be the one that Alec had used on him: *You were a saint*. Alec's compliments always came with a killer edge, a cutting undercurrent, just enough whiplash to make you wish he had kept quiet. *You were a saint*, Alec had said. *Were*. Past tense. Just like Alec, the professor, to insult people by changing the tense of his verbs.

"What happened with Alec?" Harold asked.

"I surprised him outside the club."

"That's nice. Did you go to a hotel?"

"Yes."

"Did you stay over?"

"Yes."

Harold lit a new cigarette. His stomach was throbbing painfully. He sat unmoving as Francine reached into his pocket, took out his cigarettes. He waited until she was ready, then whipped out his lighter and held it to her cigarette with a ceremonial snap, the way he used to when they first met.

Francine went back to her chair. Her head dipped again, turning her hair into an iridescent golden crown.

"Is he going back to the hotel tonight?"

"That one or somewhere else."

"I think I'll have a sleep before dinner," Harold said. When Harold woke, Francine was gone. He stood up. His skin was cool smooth, gleaming, dead. Fresh clothes had been laid out. When he opened the curtains he saw that it was night. The black attaché case was standing in the centre of the floor, waiting. Harold picked it up. Then, pushing the window open, he slid out into the cool air, drifted down to the street. Through the lit windows of restaurants he could see people eating, their bottles of wine and sparkling water gleaming, their heads bobbing as they raised their forks, and offered each other their shining faces, their warm mouths.

When he arrived at the club it was already filled with smoke and noise. Francine was at their usual table and as he joined her Elvis came on stage. He was in a white sailor's costume, his bulky shirt billowing like a sail with a bellyful of wind. His low voice coughed up a few loose rumbles as the first chords rolled out of his guitar.

"Have a good sleep?"

"Never felt better."

> Had a dog who wore a wig
> Danced the polka like a pig
> Loved a bitch who let him down
> Lost his life in a dusty town

2

I was dreaming that I was back in my old life, the life I used to believe I was living, back in my own house, standing at the door of my own bedroom, watching Margaret sleep. Beside her lay a man staring into the darkness. Suddenly I woke up. I reached for the light. Harold was sitting on a chair near the window.

"You."

"Me."

The hotel room was small, the bedside lamp a maroon ceramic cherub kicking his round little toes into the damp air.

"Nice pyjamas," Harold said.

"Thanks." I was wearing the thin cotton jogging pants Harold had given me years ago, the memento of a high school reunion Harold had gone to while I made an excuse to stay home. Now I picked up a T-shirt from the end of the bed, pulled it on. It also was a gift from Harold, from Disneyland.

Harold was sitting stiffly, his suit jacket folded neatly on his lap, as though he were the mourner and I the dead man, as though he had been there for hours, watching the body for signs the soul might be about to migrate.

"How's it going?" Harold asked.

"Not so well."

Harold nodded as though to confirm he knew what had happened, as though to let me know it would be unlucky to talk about it aloud. Anything put into words was reduced, doomed, shrunk into insignificance.

> Tell her I love her
> Tell her I care
> Tell her my tongue
> Died in my lung
> Tell her my pockets are empty

Harold's eyes had a faint smile, the smile he used to have when everything was smooth and mellow and drifting along with the music. He reached into his folded coat, pulled out a cigarette, stood it like a tiny gymnast on the tip of his finger, flipped it high into the air. "Three and a half twists," Harold said. The cigarette reached its apogee, hung suspended in the air long enough for me to imagine us in a cheap Western movie, in the midst of a dusty nowhere, Harold doing his trick and I, while the cigarette defied gravity, drawing my gun to blast that cancer-causing tobacco villain into another universe. But we weren't in a cheap Western movie, in the midst of a dusty nowhere. We were in a cheap downtown Toronto hotel room and after the cigarette had briefly hovered, it started its descent. Once, twice, three times it somersaulted — then half-way through the fourth it landed, filter-tip down, in the centre of Harold's palm.

"Well done," Harold said to the cigarette. "Now I'm going to smoke you."

"Ingrate."

"You see — you're too sentimental. You get too attach-ed," Harold said. But he put the gymnastic cigarette in his shirt pocket, drew out another one.

"How did you do it, anyway? Is there a whole world of dead people out there?"

"I don't know. I just showed up. There I was. I just do what I do."

"And you can do whatever you want?"

"No. Things start to fade out if I make the wrong move."

Harold said this in an unexpectedly soft voice, and his eyes filled with tears. "Sometimes I like it."

"And Francine?"

"I don't know." Harold's tears were coming faster now; he had one hand up, over his face. He was crying and talking at the same time but I couldn't move, couldn't understand, couldn't do anything but watch. Like the last months of Harold's dying, when I and the others could only try to smooth the collapse of Harold's body while Harold, the *real* Harold, struggled to get free.

After a while Harold stopped crying. His face was dark and shining with distress. One July night near the end, when Francine was away, Harold and I were alone in what had been a long semi-comatose silence, lasting from late afternoon until the sky emptied to a hollow glassy blue and the first stars were beginning to show; this was after Harold had gone blind so when I was alone with him I often didn't bother to turn on the lights.

Suddenly Harold said, his voice clearer than it had been for months, "Alec. You have to do something about the pain."

"More drugs?"

"The drugs aren't working." He turned towards me. His blind eyes. His cheeks consumed by cancer and pain. "Not working," he repeated, his voice ringing with the old persuasive certainty. "Alec, I really can't stand this. They told me I was going to die, but they didn't tell me how much it would hurt."

I was holding his hands. He was gripping back. Hard. Somehow he had managed to push the pain away for a few seconds, return to himself in order to solve this insoluble problem.

"More drugs would be better," I said.

A silence. One which, I knew, I was free to interpret as meaning that Harold was considering this proposition. But then he shut his eyes, always his signal that what had been said was beneath consideration.

But I persisted. "Do you want me to get them right away? Right now?"

This time the pause was brief, followed by a sigh.

"Could you?" His voice wavering.

"I promise," I said, putting my hand on Harold's shoulder. I had to promise. After all, Harold had to be sick, had to be dying in agony, had to be suffering unbearable pain, hallucinations, delusions. The least I could do was make a promise and keep it.

"I'm going to call the hospital now," I said. By the time I finished Harold was clawing at the bars, rocking back and forth as he moaned and cursed. Two hours of ever-mounting anguish. When the nurse arrived she first gave Harold an injection; then she strapped a morphine pump into place, its needle sunk and bandaged into his belly. Now Harold had gone one more step. No one would ever again pretend to worry that too many morphine pills would make him an addict. Harold wasn't going to have any more morphine pills. From now on, any time he wanted, Harold could press a button that would shoot liquid morphine directly into his bloodstream. Seconds later his brain would light up, spine snap into service as a zillion-fibre telephone line humming with happy messages transformed his nervous system into a midway of joy. At least that was the plan. I had kept my promise. Now Harold would escape the tyranny of pain. But something went wrong. Harold had escaped, but to where? He was lying unconscious, face utterly slack, arms limp, stunned by the morphine and exhausted by the pain he had endured, the pain he had not been able to endure. He didn't look happy, he looked dead.

"Sometimes when they're like this they sleep for a long time," the nurse said.

They. "Like for ever?" I asked — but the nurse pretended she hadn't heard.

"I'm sorry about the other night in the kitchen," I now said. "I was so surprised."

"You were the only brother I had," Harold said.

"Same here."

We sat for a moment. Harold's face slowly composed itself. He got up and opened the window. From somewhere came the clanking and whine of a snowplough. "Christ," Harold said, "this place is depressing. Are we going to sit here all night or should we go out and get a drink?"

"A drink? It's —"

"My bar is always open." Harold grinned, snapped his fingers, lit his cigarette. As I got off the bed I could feel the juice flowing through my body, the strange post-mortal current Harold had switched on in me at Club Elvis. I stretched just to feel that juice in my spine, flooding my muscles. Maybe this was the way Harold had felt after those big hits of morphine that left him looking boneless and deflated.

A few moments later we were outside. Suddenly we were free. It was as though we were teenagers again, liberated from the house and off for a late-night adventure.

Soon we were heading down Queen Street. The past few days had been bitterly cold but now the weather was changing and a warm melting wind was rising from the southwest. The street was layered with the smells of moisture, thawing garbage, the crushed detritus of the Chinese market.

Club Elvis was firmly in place, the red CLUB ELVIS letters rhythmically pulsing into the street. This time there was no hesitation. Harold at my side I strode down the narrow pathway into the smoky room full of drinkers, loud with late-night shouts and boasts and music pounding from the giant jukebox that had been wheeled into the centre of the stage. In a front corner, at a table half in shadows, sat the main Elvis, the huge one with the long oiled black hair and the deep velvety voice. The Nymphets were on either side of him, their table was cluttered with bottles and platters of food. As Harold and I sat down the Elvis looked up, raised his hand to Harold, who returned the wave and nodded.

The noise began to fade. The drinkers, I now noticed, were mostly sipping at cocktails or wine. Each table had its own pool of amber light, emanating from a lamp made out of a bottle with a shade. Our bottle, I now saw, was Chianti. Maybe it was Italian night. Elvis was wearing some sort of black cape. The Nymphets had on dark stylish dresses and with each of their movements jewellery flashed across the darkness. A waiter appeared carrying a tray with two glasses and a bottle of grappa. His black pants had a knife-edge crease, his white jacket was of thick soft linen. Bowing ceremoniously he plonked down the glasses. *Signori*. Then he filled them, clicked his heels with a smile and left.

Various great lines have been written about how wood turns to ash, love to bitterness, etc. One of those would be useful to express how the sweet gold power that had surged through me as we left the hotel had now turned to something else, not its absence but a dark premonitory rush.

"So," Harold said. "This is it."

"It?"

"I mean," Harold said, "as they say, we can't keep meeting like this."

"You mean we've used up all the good waiters?"

Harold ignored this. Harold's broad moustache. His eyebrows raised the way they used to when he wanted to make a point — or a joke. The dark hair of his eyebrows and moustache and the new post-illness silver at his temples. Harold's grey-green eyes, unchanged, waiting.

The waiter reappeared, poured another round of grappa. Now the *Goldberg Variations* — my mother was the first to buy Harold this record, back when there were records — filtered softly through the speakers.

"Great stuff," Harold said.

A sudden tumble of treble notes, a bass counterpoint, Glenn Gould's breathing across the microphone, across time, across death.

"I did love you," I said.

"I know."

The orderly progression of necessary harmonies. Repetitions and variations. The necessary building to the unavoidable climax.

Harold's eyes still waiting for something from me. Green eyes that could slide from being hard and needing to soft and listening. Harold's eyes that he liked to show and liked to hide. The day the doctor slowly moved her hand in front of Harold's eyes, asking him how many fingers and Harold's dead quiet voice: "None." Harold's blind dreams of seeing.

"*Santé*," Harold said, lifting his glass.

We drank.

"And for you?" I asked. "What toast can I offer you?"

We had twisted our chairs so we were looking out on the spectacle of Club Elvis. As though we were watching a television show, sitting at the end of a dock taking in a sunset, standing on a Paris bridge reading our fortunes in the fog, or watching ourselves travelling in a time machine back to our past, our pre-illness, pre-Margaret, pre-Francine, pre-historic brother club past — back to schooldays ruled by monster-faced teachers, back to lunches that smelled of stale eggs and dried rubbery carrots, back to leaky rowboats, boots filled with snow, to me looking down to Harold in a patch of sunlight and seeing his baby eyes locked into mine.

Coffee arrived. I lit one of Harold's cigarettes.

"Offer me life," Harold said, "I don't want to die." He had turned completely white and he was leaning forward, his eyes closed. Then he fell off his chair onto the floor.

I was kneeling beside him when the Elvis arrived. He bent over Harold, he took Harold's face in his huge soft hands. "Brother ghost," his voice rumbled, "come back brother ghost." Harold's eyes opened. The Elvis reached into Harold's jacket for a vial of pills. I placed one on the tip of Harold's tongue — the way I used to so he could feel to make sure he was being given the pills he knew, not some concoction designed to kill him. Then the vial fell from my trembling hands and I had to get down and scoop everything from the floor. The Elvis pulled Harold up, helped him into his chair, then faded back to his table as Harold started drinking coffee.

"You okay?" I asked.

"Get serious." Harold stood, picked up his black attaché case and put a small pile of crisp banknotes on the table. He looked tired, but tired in an ordinary way, tired in the way he always looked when we'd stayed up late drinking, getting to the bottom of the bottle, getting tired waiting for whatever was supposed to happen, for the ritual that had once been full, waiting for the time machine, waiting until we could go to bed having worshipped at the altar of something we'd both once touched.

Standing outside Club Elvis we did a strange thing. We shook hands. It was a long time since I'd felt Harold's hand. The last time I'd held it, he was lying dead in the hospital bed he had thought was a drawer or a coffin.

"Goodnight brother," Harold now said. But he didn't move and neither did I. Harold shrugged. "Good," he said. "I was hoping you would come."

"Where are we going?"

"Follow me."

He began walking. The air was raw and warming, the snow melting, and the soles of our shoes slapped against the wet pavement. Despite the fact that I was slightly shorter we were walking in an exact matched rhythm, the way as children we'd perfected matching our steps together as we snuck downstairs for a midnight snack.

At the traffic lights Harold flagged a cab. "Jewish cemetery," he said, and before the driver could ask which one, Harold told him where it was.

When we arrived Harold watched the taxi until it had disappeared around a corner. "Probably thinks we're Nazis," Harold said.

The entrance was a stone arch with a heavy metal gate.

Harold took a key out of his pocket, made me light matches while he found the lock.

Inside we moved slowly among the gravestones. When Harold got to his own he stopped and put down his attaché case.

He turned and looked at me. There was a moon. Just a crescent, enough to light up Harold's eyes and glint off the spades waiting to be used.

I lit another match, held it in front of the gravestone to read the inscription.

"Don't worry. It's mine."

Harold Constantine

1954–1992

Always Remembered

"Are you down there?"

"Of course not," Harold said. "I'm right here."

"So?"

"Get digging."

"I don't want to."

"You have to."

I took off my coat, folded it carefully and put it on a nearby headstone. In the snow I outlined the rectangle that needed to be dug. The snow was melting and when I tapped the ground with the shovel I could hear the thin echo ground makes when it is topped by a frozen crust.

The first thing I did was to cut away the turf. When it was in a neat pile I started to dig deeper. After a while Harold opened the attaché case. It was his old magic case but now it contained two bottles of grappa, side by side, lying on a white linen shroud. Harold took out one of the bottles. We had a drink.

"This is ridiculous," I said. "We haven't settled anything. What about Francine? What about everyone? Aren't we going to play Rosencrantz and Guildenstern? We still haven't really *talked*."

"No time."

The earth was dark and heavy, laced with smooth stones almost the size of skulls. Some of them rolled off the mound of fresh-dug earth and lay like moons in the melting snow.

Harold is so thin. He is keeping me company, digging along, but each time he raises the shovel it holds only a few grains of dirt. That's all right with me, I want this to last for ever, but just as I'm trying to stretch it out, my spade hits the coffin. We're down so deep I can't see the snow any more, just the bank of raw earth surrounding the grave.

Now Harold works faster, with a few quick movements he has the coffin clearly exposed.

He gives his grin, his big shit-eating grin that makes his moustache fan out across his face. Then he kneels on the coffin and knocks. A hollow sound. Before I can stop him he pulls the lid open.

"Aah," Harold says.

The coffin is empty, except for the scent of fresh pine, which rises into our faces. Harold clambers up to the surface, holds his hand out to help me.

Harold has Alec's hand. It would be so easy to push Alec into the coffin meant for him. He sees himself bent over Alec, sees the terror writing itself on Alec's face as he realizes what is to come. He hears Alec's shouts of protest as the lid slams shut — BANG!! — then earth and stones thunder down.

"This is the hard part," Harold says. He pulls Alec out of the grave and Alec is standing beside him.

Harold takes off his jacket, his pants, his shoes and socks, his shirt, his underwear. With his right hand he reaches under his left armpit and begins peeling away his skin. It comes off in thick warm strips, hot and excited, eager to be shed. When he's done it lies around his ankles, heavy pink-white coils that glisten in the moonlight. He bends over, throws it into the coffin. Muscles, tendons, organs, everything but his skeleton follows. The last to go are his eyes, which he tosses on top of the gleaming entrails. Now the wind is blowing hard, blowing his skeleton white and bleached as any worm-eaten sun-dried derelict. Even as they watch, the coffin empties out and the wood turns grey and spongy.

"Goodbye," Harold says to Alec. "I forgive you. For everything."

"Thank you," Alec says. "I forgive you."

I am standing above my brother's coffin, holding Harold's skeleton in my arms. *I forgive you. For dying.* Finally I realize there are no more last words, no more decisions. Kneeling, I lay my brother in his coffin. "Goodbye," I say. "Thank you." Onto his bones I throw the white linen shroud, the burial cloth of our ancestors. It floats slowly through the night air, settles over Harold. As it begins to disintegrate I put in his black Italian suit, the unopened bottle of grappa. I close the lid. I shovel until the grave is full.

Harold lay in the coffin. This, he thought to himself, is the kind of situation a man spends his whole life avoiding. Very funny. He could hear his brother above him, feel him kneeling on the grave, putting the turf back into place. The task suited Alec, he had worked as a gardener for a few summers. Each square was delicately smoothed and patted.

He could hear Alec gulping at the grappa. He felt for his own bottle. Alec was standing up now. Harold could see him, erect in the moonlight, brushing the attaché case clean. Harold closed his eyes. For a moment Harold felt himself rising, rising through the heavy earth and the damp air, rising to reappear at Alec's side.

But nothing happened. He was just there, in his coffin, in the darkness, listening to Alec breathe, waiting for the slow muffled sound of his brother's receding footsteps.

I am leaning over my brother's grave. The earth black under the moon's silver crescent. A rush of wind cracks the branches of an unseen tree. The echo of birds' wings.

I set down the shovel. The air is cool on my face, sweet and promising. It seems for ever since I've stood outside, felt sweet spring air against my skin, felt the sweetness of spring offering to seep into me. I rub the dirt from my hands. The attaché case, Harold's case, is lying open in the snow. I kneel down beside it. Then I put my ear to the grave, listening for Harold. I hear the deep hum of some-thing — the city, the grinding motors of transport trucks, the subterranean twang of a guitar string, the vibration of Harold's bones.

"To you, Harold," I say, taking a last drink.

I close the case, and without looking back I walk away from the grave.

On the other side of the cemetery gate, Francine is waiting. I come out and she holds the case as I work the latch back into place. Now it is the way we found it — a stone arch, a heavy rusted gate, a view into a blurred dark cemetery where nothing is distinct.

We wander through the city. I can't imagine touching her now. That was another lifetime, a non-life, a mirage we both needed.

We are sitting on a stone bench in a mid-town park not so far from where Francine used to live, in that other life-time, that non-life ago. Francine drinks grappa with me. She looks wild — her tawny hair, the light in her eyes, most of all her lips and mouth, as though her face has taken on the new savage shape of everything unspoken.

Slowly the moon works its way across our small sky. Its light is above us but its light also burns from the centre of the bottle we are passing back and forth, along with various provisional memories slowly melting into the stone.

E are at the cabin and the May grass is a dense incandescent green. Last night we slept with the windows open. The spring air invaded our bed, our skin, melted Margaret and me together in this hopeful new season we are starting to trust.

I woke just as the sun began to rise. So bursting with spring, with happiness to be here, that I had to go outside, walk through the muddy fields, past the pine groves and the patches of poplar with their tiny new lime-green leaves, the clusters of trilliums, the dark exploding green of the moss, the dogwood blossoms, to the beaver pond, the big mounded house covered with mud-sealed branches.

On the other side of that pond is a steep hill dotted with towering maples. In May those maples have only the beginnings of leaves, their still-bare branches stretch urgently into the morning sky, desperately sucking in spring warmth and light. Birds perch in the spaces that soon will be thick with leaves. Their songs carry through the last emptiness of winter; they fly intricate loops in spaces that are getting ready to disappear.

A lifetime ago, Harold and I sat on that hill.

It was summer, full summer, juicy with greenness, the sounds of frogs, birds, insects, the soaking long grass to our knees, rain dripping from the canopy of leaves under which we had taken shelter.

Harold was wearing a bush jacket I had loaned him against the rain, and on his head Herr Meyser. Back then, lifetimes ago, Harold's lifetime ago and also before my children had been born, conceived, even thought of, back when Elvis and everyone else were alive for the first time, Harold's dark hair grew thick and long, his moustache bushy, his eyes glittered. He was wearing my bush jacket, Herr Meyser, and the rain and wet grass had soaked his jeans to the thighs.

I, too, was soaked. My running shoes were filled with water and mud. On my head rode a Mexican straw hat bought that very day at the general store. And since Harold had on my jacket I was wearing his, a dark brown corduroy masterpiece with enviable black leather trim on the cuffs and outside pockets, a satin-lined two-button sports coat I so frequently admired that he broke down and gave it to me.

On that day, lifetimes ago, we stepped out of the cabin and there were no signs of rain.

An hour later we were surrounded by rain falling and rain dripping, rain pattering on the leaves above us and onto the ruffled surface of the pond. The splash of frogs occasionally remembering we were there. Rainy bird songs. Leaves dumping their loads on each other. Wet rushes of wind.

"I dare you to roll down the hill," said Harold.

From the crest, where we were sitting, to the pond, was a stretch I had often skied. Eventually my children would ski it. Of course I didn't know that. Nor did I know I would one day sit across from myself, watching the way, lifetimes ago, I surveyed the hundred feet or so that led down to the water.

I tried to lay out a course that would avoid the biggest rocks. That summer, lifetimes ago, the juniper bushes that now spread over the grass were small spikey sentinels. The grass, I noted, was long, which meant there were no recent cowpies. I looked across the pond to the place where I would eventually sit and remember. Yes, I did that. It would be interesting to claim that even then I saw my future self, that a sudden shadow passed across the sky, a crow through the branches, an omen. But all I saw was a huge granite outcropping with small pine trees — Christmas-tree-size trees now tall enough that I've lopped their branches and can walk in the thick needled grove beneath — and nothing else. No future self. No warning.

I took off my glasses and put them in the satin-lined inside pocket of Harold's thick corduroy jacket. I folded my arms across my chest to protect the glasses. Then I lay down and started to roll. At first it was just a series of bumps. Then the bumps smoothed out, I opened my eyes and as I rolled I caught blurred flashes of sky, trees, empty rock across the pond. My insides and outsides were spinning at wildly different rates. By the time I hit the water I had forgotten everything but the sensation of motion, the bumpy grassy-buffered massage of the hill, the sweet smell of dandelions and grass and lilac mixed with the dank muddy odour of otter and beaver. I was on my back, half my body in the water, one hand and arm bobbing with the small waves. Somehow my head had come to rest on a comfortable hummock of earth. Everything felt whole, perfect, protected. Drops of water fell on my face, pooled around my eyes, ran in and out of my nostrils. The earth pulsed to the beating of my heart. Eventually I stood, shook out Harold's jacket. Harold was lying part way down the hill, his arms outstretched, his mouth arched open to receive the rain.